MURDERED BY NATURE

MURDERED BY NATURE

Roderic Jeffries

This first world edition published 2012
in Great Britain and in the USA by
SEVERN HOUSE PUBLISHERS LTD of
9–15 High Street, Sutton, Surrey, England, SM1 1DF.

British Library Cataloguing in Publication Data

Jeffries, Roderic, 1926-
  Murdered by nature. – (An Inspector Alvarez mystery)
  1. Alvarez, Enrique (Fictitious character)–Fiction.
  2. Police–Spain–Majorca–Fiction. 3. Detective and
  mystery stories.
  I. Title II. Series
  823.9'14-dc23   SEP   2012

ISBN-13: 978-0-7278-8147-2 (cased)

All Severn House titles are printed on acid-free paper.

Severn House Publishers support The Forest Stewardship Council [FSC], the
leading international forest certification organisation. All our titles that are
printed on Greenpeace-approved FSC-certified paper carry the FSC logo.

MIX
Paper from
responsible sources
FSC
www.fsc.org   FSC® C018575

Typeset by Palimpsest Book Production Ltd.,
Falkirk, Stirlingshire, Scotland.
Printed and bound in Great Britain by
MPG Books Ltd., Bodmin, Cornwall.

Dedicated to X.K.J.

ONE

The sunshine, warm for October, reached through the unshuttered window on the first floor of the office in the Guardia Civil post in Llueso. It awoke Alvarez. As his mind reassembled, he was surprised he had been asleep; it was still Friday morning.

He watched the drift of dust in the sunshine. No one had interrupted his stolen sleep. Dolores was in a good mood and for supper the previous evening had cooked *Calamares con anchoas en cocotte* – rings of squid, olive oil, garlic, tomatoes, white wine, anchovies, seasoning. Delicious! Superior Chief Salas was on holiday, there was a lack of crime in the area, and the local government's proposal to increase the tax on alcohol had been defeated by members who understood a man who could not afford a coñac and a glass or two of wine was deprived of both contentment and any intention to vote for the existing government at the next election.

Life sometimes was generous.

Laura entered the bedroom. As she passed the bed on which her husband had lain, fresh tears ran down her cheeks. She went over to the picture window and stared out at the bay, sight blurred until she rubbed her eyes.

A motor cruiser – gin palace, Charles would have called her – was passing the face of the rock promontory, Roca Nesca, closer than was advisable. Charles would have shouted and waved his hands to tell the landlubber at the helm to alter course. *Eos*, Charles' ketch, maintained in prime condition, was moored alongside the landing stage. As she looked at her, her thoughts drifted . . .

They had been sailing to Monte Carlo when they'd been caught in a sudden Mediterranean storm. '*Eos*' sons having fun,' he'd called out as heavy spray and sheets of sea had lashed him at the helm. At his command – and in a boat, he was very much in command – she had taken shelter in the cabin. From there, she had watched as he eased them through the challenging water and understood he was excited, not scared; she had lost some of her own fear . . .

There was a knock on the door. She called out.

Beatriz stepped in. 'Señora, I have cooked—'

'I don't want anything.'

'You must eat.'

'Not now.'

Beatriz tried to persuade her to eat the meal so carefully prepared. She wanted to shout 'shut up', remained silent, knowing Beatriz was trying to help in the only way in which she thought it right to do so.

Beatriz left. Laura looked out at the bay again. The motor cruiser was now heading east, away from Roca Nesca . . .

The coffee machine in the nurses' room had malfunctioned for over a week and one attempt to mend it had failed. She had been mixing a cup of Nescafé when Frieda entered.

'I was hoping someone would be here because I forgot to buy another pot of instant. Don't mind lending me a spoonful, do you?' Frieda asked.

'Help yourself.'

'Heard the latest?' she asked as she picked up the jar.

'Depends what that is.'

'Charles Ashton and his wife have been brought in after a car crash; he should last, but she probably won't.'

'Who are they?'

'You live in another world . . .! I've run out of sugar too. Do you mind?'

She wondered if Frieda ever bothered to buy coffee or sugar as she passed across a plastic container.

'He was a big noise in some company and retired with a huge bonus and a pension that would keep us in sable; there was a row about it in Parliament. Not that that lot have anything to shout about when they lead the lives of Riley with all the expenses' fiddling.'

On the second day after Charles' admission, she had been told to attend to his dressings. She had expected to meet a hawk-eyed man of an abrupt nature. He had been crying because he had just learned his wife had died despite every effort to keep her alive.

She could and should have done no more than speak words of condolence, but had learned the pain of tragedy. After saving for two years, her parents had flown to Malaya to visit the grave of her mother's father. The plane had crashed, killing passengers and crew. Her aunt and uncle had 'adopted' her. Their kindness had blunted her misery, not erased it. She sat on the bed and held Charles lightly against herself.

The sister had entered the room and, outraged by the breach of nursing/patient relationship, had angrily ordered Laura out of the room. Charles had contradicted her so sharply, she had momentarily stood there, bewildered, before she had hurried out.

He had discharged himself, against his surgeon's advice. He had asked that Laura return with him to his Chelsea home as his private nurse. He had been told that was impossible. Within a short time, it had become possible. That was her first practical understanding of the power of wealth and authority.

After several weeks, when he had recovered fully, she had said to him: 'I must return to the hospital or they'll have forgotten who I am and I'll be looking for another job.'

'I arranged they accept you back when you leave here.'

'Then I'll get in touch with them . . .'

'You're in a hurry to get away?'

'It's not a question of what *I* want to do.'

'It's always just that question.'

She occasionally twitted him. 'You're very chairman and chief executive this morning.'

'Do you usually live with your parents?'

She did not immediately understand the reason for his question. 'My parents were lost in a plane crash.'

'A long time ago?'

'Not very. Is there something more you want?'

'For you to explain why you physically comforted me contrary to the cast-iron rule against emotional nursing.'

'Why d'you ask?'

'Answer my question first.'

The note of command in his voice annoyed her and she spoke aggressively. 'You were shocked and despairing because you'd learned that tragically your wife had died. I reckoned if I could bring you some relief with a hug, I'd do a lot more good than any condolences.'

'No other nurse would have considered such action.'

'You can't say that.'

'You imagined another, to help a stranger, would have dared brave authority's wrath and the probability of a damning accusation?'

'Yes.'

'You are a danger to yourself. Will you stay here?'

'No.'

'I am being . . . What did you call me? So very chairman and chief executive?'

'I have to work.'

'Not if you marry me.'

In their weeks together, they had gained and enjoyed a strong friendship, but she did not read women's novels and see stars in a cloud-covered sky.

'Laura, when they told me Belinda had died, I wished I had died with her. You taught me there could be release from tragedy. Will you marry me?'

'No.'

'Why not?'

She had hurried out of the room. The next day, she had packed her bag and was carrying it out of the bedroom when a maid insisted on taking it from her. Downstairs, she'd gone into the sitting room to say goodbye to Charles. He had again proposed to her; she had again refused. He was not a man who found it easy to express his emotions, but he tried to make her understand that she would be offering him the love and affection he thought he had lost forever when his wife died.

She had tried to find a reason for refusal which he would accept. She lived with her uncle and aunt in a semi-detached house in suburban London. Their lives were of necessity economical. Once a year, they travelled to Italy on a package holiday. He owned houses in London, Mallorca, the Bahamian Islands, and had a flat in New York. 'Yours is a different world.'

'Explore it.'

'No.'

'You'll fit in perfectly.'

'You should marry someone who's used to luxury, wears fashionable clothes, isn't likely to be socially all at sea.'

'You can adjust to anything because you are *you*.'

'There's quite a difference in our ages.'

'So?'

'It's . . .' She hesitated, then said in a rush of words: 'People will say I'm marrying you for your money.'

'More fool them if they can't understand you are a woman who could never sell herself.'

'But . . . I don't know if I could fit into your life.'

'Mrs Wright said, after you told her you were leaving, that the staff would be very sorry. You've gained their willing acceptance and there's no greater compliment, no stronger argument to contradict your fears.'

'I find it . . . well, disturbingly odd to be driven around in a chauffeured car, difficult to accept the obsequiousness of waiters. There's seldom a price on the menu I'm given so I always wonder if I ought to have chosen something cheaper.'

'You will learn how to overcome such problems.'

TWO

They had honeymooned in Grand Bahama, returned to London, flown to Mallorca. Son Dragó was a graceful house, sited on the peninsula of Roca Nesca, its sides up to six metres above the water. Charles would have renamed the estate Roca Nube Diez had he not disliked tampering with tradition.

He had shown her Mallorca, the areas of dramatic grandeur and of quiet beauty. They had walked in the mountainous interior, a foreign land to tourists; explored hidden valleys; spoken to those who lived in isolated homes and had been offered hospitality, however slight, as was the custom; had become 'lost' in pine forests which offered that rare pleasure, utter peace.

Charles had said they'd go in search of Mosques grosses, wild orchids said to grow on Puig Flexa d'Or.

'Arrow of gold is an odd name for a mountain.'

He'd poured out Krug for her, for himself, settled in a chair. 'It's an interesting story how it came to be named. Back in the eighteenth century, it was owned by Don Igcaray, one of the wealthiest landlords on the island and a nasty individual.

'Tolo worked for him as a shepherd. He was semi-literate – his family had not been able to afford to send him to school – and had managed the flock for many years. One day, he found the prize ram was missing. He searched until dark and it was the next morning before he admitted the loss. Don Igcaray responded in the manner to be expected of such a man. He accused Tolo of negligence, of cheating him by selling the ram, of passing it on to a neighbour for servicing at many pesetas a ewe, of butchering it to eat. If the ram was not found quickly, Tolo would be charged with theft, found guilty, imprisoned. No meaningless threat because, in those days, wealthy landlords administered their own justice.

'His mind knowing only fear – imprisonment would mean poverty for his wife and children – Tolo had risen before dawn and begun his new search as daylight appeared. By nightfall, he had failed to find the ram. Too weary to return to his small, primitively furnished *caseta*, he had found a hollow, curled up in this and, despite the cold and his fears – evil spirits were abroad at night; how could he possibly avoid the consequences of Igcaray's malevolent anger? – slept until he was awakened by a golden arrow of light, the head of which pointed to a neighbour's land. At dawn, he went down the mountain and across to the neighbour's land and in a dense bramble thicket, found the ram, held fast after blundering its way into the thicket for a reason only a sheep could explain. The mountain became known as Flexa d'Or.'

'People believed the story?'

'Why not, when it offered the hope of celestial assistance?'

They drove around the bay to Puig Flexa d'Or. They searched without success for the tightly bunched, blue, white, and red orchids until they were too hot and tired to continue. 'We didn't deserve a golden arrow,' he remarked as they returned to the car.

Half an hour later, they arrived at Son Dragó. A large house with five bedrooms and en-suite bathrooms, library, large and small sitting-rooms, breakfast, dining, computer and TV rooms, very well-equipped kitchen, store room, scullery, and full staff rooms. It had been built in traditional style, yet imbued with more grace than was customary. The architect had been Italian.

The butler, Benavides, opened the car doors for them. 'Did you have success, señor?'

'We lacked celestial assistance.' Charles spoke fluent, incorrect Spanish; Laura understood what was said, still found difficulty in speaking.

As they entered the hall, Benavides said: 'Señor, a man came here while you were away.'

She noticed he had said 'a man' instead of 'a señor', but did not immediately infer the reason for this.

'Who was he?'

'Kerr.'

'Kerr,' Charles repeated. 'No centimos dropping for the moment. Does the name mean anything to you, sweet?'

'No.' She answered too quickly, too sharply, but his dismissal of the unknown visitor persuaded her that he had not wondered if the name *might* hold significance for her.

Charles had complained of chest pains and at Laura's insistence had consulted a specialist in Palma who diagnosed a heart problem. Back home, he asked Benavides to bring up a bottle of Bollinger from the cellar.

'No,' she said. 'You heard what was advised.'

'To take life more quietly. He did not suggest I retired to a monastery.'

'But . . .'

'Is one glass of champagne going to blast me into eternity?'

Laura had gradually become able to dismiss from her mind for most of the time the possibilities which could follow Charles' heart complaint, but had asked him not to go out on his own in *Eos* when there was much wind because the effort then needed to handle her could become severe. Her words had been accepted, but had little effect, yet since he seemed untroubled by physical demands, she had not worried unduly. One evening as it was turning dark and there was considerable wind, he had said he was going to sail with García, their gardener and handyman, aboard. She and Beatriz had tried to dissuade him without success. On his return it had been clear he was very ill. She had called the specialist. He had arrived shortly before her husband had died.

THREE

The phone rang. Alvarez ignored the call. The ringing finally ceased, justifying his belief that if something was annoying, ignore it and the annoyance would cease. He looked at his watch. By his own timekeeping, not Salas', he could enjoy a mid-morning *merienda*.

He left the post, crossed the old square in which many idle tourists drank more than they should, entered Club Llueso. Roca, the bartender, walked up to where Alvarez leaned against the bar.

'What's happened this time?' Roca asked.

'Why d'you ask?'

'You almost look cheerful.'

'Life is being generous.'

'To you? Must be a mistake.'

'I'll have a coñac, a café cortado, and no comments.'

Roca activated the espresso machine, poured out a generous brandy, carried glass, cup and saucer to where Alvarez leaned. 'You won something on the lottery?'

'My superior is on holiday and so I have only myself to think about.'

'Surprised you don't look more gloomy than usual.' Roca went along the bar to serve another customer.

Alvarez drank some coffee, poured brandy into the cup. He finished the coffee, signalled to Roca. 'Another coffee and this time a man-sized coñac.'

'Doubt there's a glass in the place that'll hold that much.'

Alvarez walked away from the bar and sat on a newly vacated window seat, stared at the people on the raised portion of the square, seated in the shade of large sun-umbrellas; the changing swirl of pedestrians; a redhead in a tight fitting blouse and very short skirt.

Roca brought brandy and coffee to the table. 'Who are you lusting after today?'

'My emotion is pleasure, gained from watching people enjoy themselves.'

'I'll try to believe that.'

Twenty minutes later, Alvarez returned to the post, and as he entered his room, the phone rang.

'Inspector Alvarez?'

He identified the voice immediately. 'Yes, señorita.'

'Then you *are* working today!'

Ángela Torres had worked as Salas' secretary for so many years that she reflected his manners and assumed his authority.

'Why should you doubt that?' he asked.

'I have phoned several times without you replying.'

'There was an incident which needed my attention. A man in the supermarket – that is, the first one to be built in the Port, which was many years ago—'

'You will make your report to Comisario Borne.'

'Who?'

'You have trouble with your hearing?'

'I don't understand why I should speak to the Comisario.'

'You have not yet found time to read the notice sent to all inspectors last week?'

He looked at the medley of papers on the desk and accepted that probably amongst them was the unopened envelope. 'Señorita, I fear I have not yet received it. The post between Palma and here is often inefficient.'

'The superior chief has had reason recently to remark that perhaps it no longer exists. Comisario Borne will be acting in command until the return of Superior Chief Salas.'

Borne had the reputation of being aggressive and enjoying a high-up relative in the Cuerpo in Madrid. His mother was reputed to have been Swiss. 'He'll teach this yokel how to yodel?'

'It is interesting you consider that amusing.' She replaced the receiver.

He should have withheld the facetious comment. She would relate it to Salas on his return. Salas lacked a broad humour.

He wondered how, only a short while before, he could have viewed the world as treating him generously. Optimism was the road to disaster.

Dolores looked through the bead curtain which separated the kitchen from the living/dining room. 'Lunch is not quite ready since you have returned early.'

'I've had an exhausting morning and needed a break,' Alvarez replied.

'Only a man who believes a house looks after itself could think that exhaustion should be compensated,' his cousin said.

He leaned over and opened the door of the Mallorquin sideboard, brought out a bottle of Fundador and two glasses, set one glass in front of where Jaime, Dolores' husband, would sit. He went through to the kitchen.

'You want something?' she asked.

'Some ice.'

'And, no doubt, would like me to get it for you?'

He chose tact in preference to truth. 'Not when you're so busy.'

'I am always very busy, even if there is ever a day on which I have only the beds to make, the bedrooms to tidy, the house to dust, clean, polish, the shopping to be done, and the need to cook a tasty meal, while knowing it will be eaten with little appreciation.'

'With great appreciation.'

'Expressed with silence.'

He brought a tray of ice cubes out of the refrigerator and, as he emptied these into an ice bucket, reflected on the fact that women were, like the future, uneven and unknowable. She loved her family, was upset at the first suggestion any of them might be unwell, would defend them from the devil, yet often delivered unnecessary and illogical criticism.

He picked up the ice bucket and prepared to leave.

'You expect me to refill the ice tray and place it in the refrigerator?'

Having refilled and replaced it, he returned to the dining room, dropped four ice cubes into his glass and poured a generous brandy over them.

Jaime returned home, hurried through from the *entrada*. 'I've had one hell of a morning!'

There was a call from the kitchen. 'Another man who has been grossly overworked?'

Jaime looked at the bead curtain, then spoke to Alvarez in a low voice, necessary since, as he maintained, Dolores could hear a pin fall through the air. 'Is she uptight over something?'

'Only the usual: slaving in the house.'

'Women will find something to moan about in heaven.'

Speaking as quietly as he had, Jaime had spoken too loudly. Dolores put her head through the bead curtain. 'That something will not be the absence of men. One of you can lay the table.' She withdrew.

Sounds from the *entrada* indicated the return of Isabel and Juan from school. They entered the dining room in a rush, carried on through to the kitchen.

'There's a school visit at the end of the month,' Isabel said excitedly.

'That should be fun,' Dolores answered. 'Will you come here and stir this for a while? Juan, your shorts are dirty. What have you been doing?'

'They bet me I couldn't—' He stopped abruptly.

'What?'

'I can't remember.'

'An inherited family failing on the paternal side. Isabel, stir more quickly, and Juan, you can prepare six teeth of garlic.'

Isabel said, in a rush of words: 'Rosa's been where we're going and says it's wonderful. There's everything, and the scenic railway is so frightening, she wet her pants.'

'It is quite unnecessary to tell us that.'

'Carolina won't be able to go because of her mother,' Juan said, 'and she's spitting bloody tacks.'

'You will not use such language!'

'I've often heard Daddy say it.'

'Your father suffers from a careless tongue and when in the company of his children can find neither the desire nor the ability to curb it.'

In the dining room, Jaime refilled his glass. 'If there's an earthquake, I'll get blamed for that.'

Alvarez was dreaming he was wandering through the Mallorquin rice fields – something he had never done, in fact – when the phone awoke him. He stared at it with dislike before hauling himself upright.

'Inspector Alvarez?'

'Yes, señorita.'

'Superior Chief Salas wishes to speak to you.'

'I think you must be wrong.'

'Would you allow me to know who your caller is.'

'But I understood—'

'He will not wish to be kept waiting.'

The briefest of pauses.

'Alvarez?'

'Yes, comisario.'

'You are mistakenly yet again attempting to be humorous?'

The speaker, as he should have realized, *was* Salas. 'I'd no intention of that, señor. I thought you were Comisario Borne.'

'My secretary did not inform you who would speak to you?'

'I thought she must be wrong.'

'You had reason to accept so unlikely an event?'

'You are on holiday.'

'Unlike some, when I am in my office, I do not consider myself to be on holiday. A conference on criminality has been called by the Govern Balear. Since I am to appear before the committee, it was necessary for me to return in order to prepare the facts and figures which will be needed.'

'I don't think I can be blamed for not knowing that.'

'In the course of my preparation, I have considered the clear-up rates of the areas. It should not surprise you to learn that yours are the lowest.'

There was a silence.

Salas said sharply: 'I am waiting for an answer.'

'To what question, señor?'

'What I have just said surely makes that obvious?'

'Not exactly.'

'Then I will speak very exactly. Why does your area suffer the lowest clear-up rates?'

'It's difficult to say.'

'But simple to judge why.'

'I don't think so. I very frequently have to cope with problems because of the many foreigners who live here and the

very many who come on holiday. Foreigners bring trouble.
The English, for some reason I do not understand, are badly
affected by the sun. And having spoken to colleagues, I have
learned that that is particularly true in Port Llueso where it
seems love is in the air. They run off the rails and—'

'Are we now discussing railways?'

'I mean, they do not behave as tradition marks them.'

'In what way?'

'Men often try to have a roll in the hay, and this can cause
trouble with their wives.'

'Hardly surprising since that is something no honest man
is likely to attempt, as it would be undignified and
uncomfortable.'

'The hay is imaginary, señor. Sand is preferred, yet I think
it is probably equally uncomfortable.'

'I have yet to understand how such unwelcome, atavistic
behaviour is of consequence to the matter in hand.'

'Señor, you refer to my clear-up rate. If a husband has been
temporarily enjoying himself with another woman, his wife
sometimes expresses her annoyance physically as well as
verbally and he needs medical attention. When I later question
her about the incident, she will often deny everything, and her
husband naturally confirms her denial. He talks about a fall.
With no proof of the truth – the second woman will remain
unidentified since the husband will not have bothered to learn
her name – I can do nothing and there can be no clear-up.
Likewise, if a wife entraps another man into adultery and the
husband has cojones and finds out, he will assault the lover.
Yet none of the parties will admit anything: the husband
because he does not wish to be derided, and the other man
also doesn't want to be derided – as an incompetent lover. I
can do nothing, and the case has to be recorded as unsolved.'

'You confirm that speech introduces confusion, not clarification.' The call ended.

FOUR

The next day, Alvarez mused that the experts were right, and one did not have to travel at a vast speed to discover that time could proceed quickly or slowly. Convinced twenty minutes had passed and it would be feasible to leave the office and start the weekend, Alvarez's watch recorded there were still eight to go.

He lit a cigarette, slumped back in the chair, stared at the unshuttered window through which was visible a wall of the building on the opposite side of the road. When he had left home that morning, Dolores had been singing, and the content of her songs was always a trustworthy guide to her mood. If a blackguard, who had declared his emotional passion for a lady, had then deserted that lady, lunch would be very ordinary. If a young man, handsome, strong, brave, who throughout his absence in far-off lands had remained faithful to the maiden to whom he had declared his love, the meal would be delicious. *Filetes de salmonete en papillote?* Fillets of red mullet, green peppers, chopped dill, cream, salt cooked in foil. In her hands, a dish to earn a gourmet's praise. She might even prepare a sweet, following a custom introduced by foreigners. *Púding de castanyes.* A favourite of his. Chestnuts, butter, sugar, egg yolks, egg white, milk . . .

The phone interrupted the meal.

'Roberto Plá here.'

A policía in Playa Nueva who would not be phoning at that time of the day on a Saturday unless there was some form of trouble. 'What d'you want?' Alvarez asked, his tone expressing his resentment.

'Is life crushing your two-piece set or have you just woken up?'

'A member of the Cuerpo does not sleep when on duty.'

'And I believe in goblins. How's the family?'

It was a matter of courtesy to discuss the health of relations and mutual friends.

Plá finally gave the reason for his call during unsocial hours. 'One of the llaüts was out early, saw a body in the bay, reported it to the harbour master. He sent out a boat to bring it in. Male.'

'Any signs of trauma?'

'The doc who examined the body didn't mention any.'

'Then it's not my problem.'

'Thought you ought to know in case your superior chief asks what's going on.'

Plá had a point. 'Has the doctor anything to say about why he drowned?'

'He breathed water instead of air.'

'I can refrain from laughing.'

'The man had probably been dead for several days.'

'You mean hours.'

'Days. Takes time for the gases to bring a drowned man back to the surface. And you've only got to look at him to know he didn't drown during an early swim this morning. Skin's wrinkled and—'

'I'll take your word for it.' Alvarez seldom swam; even a very brief and partial description of the results of drowning convinced him that was with good cause. 'Anything to say who he was?'

'No. Looks like he hasn't seen much sun recently, so maybe a foreigner.'

'Age?'

'Mid twenties to early thirties won't be far wrong. One last thing: the doc says death could have been due to a cause other than drowning. So that's it. How about meeting up at a bar in the near future?'

'Fine, if this trouble doesn't keep me busy.'

'It would take more than one dead man to do that.'

Alvarez replaced the receiver, slumped back in the chair. Bad luck seemed always to strike at the most disturbing time. The unknown man had been found at the beginning of the weekend instead of after that.

He phoned Palma. Ángela Torres asked him to identify himself as if she had not known who he was from the sound of his voice. Women never missed an opportunity to suggest they were of importance.

'What is it?' Salas demanded.

'I have a report to make, señor.'

'One which, no doubt, should have been made sooner.'

'That would not have been possible since he has only just been found.'

'Some fool walker in the Tramuntana had lost himself?'

'In the bay.'

'Unless he was trying to walk across it, you have succeeded in a shorter time than usual to become virtually unintelligible.'

'He wasn't found until today.'

'As you have already stated. Will it trouble you to start your report in traditional style – that is, at the beginning?'

'A dead man was found in the bay, near the headlands, by a fishing boat this morning.'

'His identity?'

'There was no ID on him.'

'The cause of death is drowning?'

'That is uncertain.'

'Why?'

'There was no trauma, but the examining doctor thought drowning might not be the primary cause of death.'

'His grounds for that?'

'I don't know.'

'You did not think to ask him?'

'I haven't spoken to him. What information I have comes from one of the policía in Playa Nueva.'

'You saw no reason to make any further enquiries, even though you don't know the victim's name, nationality, where he had been staying, why he was in the bay?'

'Some answers can't be known until the post-mortem.'

'The time of which you do not know?'

'I imagine it will be tomorrow morning.'

'You will inform me when the time has been fixed and your imagination is unnecessary. In the meantime, you will identify the dead man.'

'That's likely to be difficult.'

'Do not allow the difficulty to prevent you making enquiries at hotels, aparthotels, and tourist holiday villas to find out if anyone is missing.'

Jaime finished his second brandy, put the glass down on the table. 'I had to work flat out all morning and then got a rollicking from the manager because I took a moment or two off for a coffee. He'd let a man work himself to death.'

'You think you're hard done by?' Alvarez asked challeng-ingly. 'I'm going to have to go back to work before lunch, then work all afternoon and evening, and it's Saturday!'

There was a call from the kitchen. 'Even though I may be kept busy from early morning until late at night, every day of the week, I offer both of you my sympathy.'

Jaime drank. He spoke in a very low voice. 'To listen to her, you'd think running a home is proper work instead of having a sit down and a coffee every half hour. She wouldn't go on like she does if it wasn't for all that women's lib nonsense.'

'And what do they think they have to liberate themselves from?'

Jaime sniggered. 'Their brassieres. I'm not objecting to that.'

Alvarez parked his car on a solid yellow line, walked into Sol y Playa aparthotel which was considerably further from the beach than the name suggested. He crossed to the office in which two young women worked. They regarded him with little interest.

'You want something?' the younger, peroxide blonde asked.

'Cuerpo,' he answered.

They were surprised, but not concerned, and their manner remained offhand. Years before, their predecessors would have been attentive and eager to assist. Democracy denigrated the forces of authority. 'I need to know if one of your guests appears to have gone missing.'

'What d'you mean?'

Modern youth enjoyed good education, but that did not improve their intelligence. 'To your knowledge, has one of your male guests disappeared between three and six days ago?'

'How are we supposed to know that?'

'Has a room not been occupied; has someone not been seen in the restaurant after previously eating there regularly?'

'We don't do rooms,' said the blonde.

'We don't eat in the dining room,' said the older, black-haired woman. It sounded as if she would have regarded it as demeaning had she done so.

'Where's the manager's office?'

The blonde pointed. On the opposite side of the square reception area was a door on which was painted 'Manager'.

He silently swore because he had not noticed the notice and must appear gormless to have needed to ask.

The manager was relatively young; the lines on his round face expressed uncertainty and weakness. He was one of the few men in the port dressed in a suit, and despite the air conditioning, his forehead and neck carried beads of sweat.

Why the hell didn't he take off the coat and tie? Alvarez wondered. Imagined they provided him with authority? He introduced himself.

'Pedro Sardagne. More trouble?'

'You've been having some?'

'If I have a day with no more than a drunk trying to break up everything and a woman screaming because she hopes someone tried to get into her bedroom, I'm in luck. Whatever the problem, you'll have a drink?'

Alvarez's opinion of the manager greatly improved. 'If you insist.'

'What would you like?'

'Coñac with just ice will go down a treat.'

Over the internal phone, Sardagne ordered one brandy with ice, one orange juice. He noticed Alvarez's surprise. 'If I had a hard drink every time I'm driven mad by the clients, I'd be taken out of here in a coffin.'

'Things are as bad as that?'

'This morning, one of the male guests has been annoying local females; the policía came along and behaved as if it was my fault. I told them, I don't know why he's on the prowl when there are a dozen young ladies staying here who likely don't want to be ladies.'

'Looking for variety?'

'Anything's possible.'

There was a knock on the door and a waitress entered. At

the manager's instructions, he handed Alvarez a glass, put the orange juice on the desk, left.

The quantity of brandy was generous, the quality superior to that which would be offered to the tourists.

'Are you here, inspector, because of visitors not paying for their drinks, nicking things from shops, drunken behaviour?'

'One dead man.'

'Makes a change.'

'He's possibly a tourist because of the whiteness of his skin, and that's as far as we can go. Picked out of the sea and no ID. I have to find out who's missing.'

'You want to know if one of our guests is? That's going to be difficult.'

Which was what he had told Salas. Sardagne had staff to do the work. 'Has a bedroom gone unoccupied?'

'One empty bed usually means another is doubly occupied.'

'The room will have been unused for at least three days. It'll have been tidy, the bed won't have been slept in. The maid will have noticed.'

'You credit them with an interest in their job?'

'I'd like to question them.'

'I suppose you want me to organize things?'

'If you don't mind.'

'Doubt it counts if I do. But it won't be the first time the day's routine gets upset.'

Since Alvarez's day had been ruined, he knew little sympathy for the other.

Maids were individually called to the office. Teresa was the first. She was taller and thinner than a woman like her would have been fifty years before, due to the better diet that prosperity had brought.

'The inspector wants to ask you something,' Sardagne said.

She faced Alvarez.

'A man, possibly a foreigner, has been found dead in the bay. There's no way of directly identifying him, so we're having to do that indirectly. Does any bedroom you deal with seem to have become unoccupied?'

'All the beds have been slept in.'

'And the rooms have shown signs of use?'

'In the usual mess. Seems like some of them haven't lived in a decent home.'

'You've no reason to think someone who was staying here at the end of last week or beginning of this one has disappeared?'

'No.'

Seven more maids provided equally negative reports.

'I'll have a word with the restaurant staff,' Alvarez said as the last maid left the office.

Sardagne complained weakly. 'They'll all be extremely busy at this time of morning.'

'I'll not keep them away from work any longer than necessary.'

None of the waiters had served a guest who would have been expected to continue to eat in the restaurant, but who had failed to do so.

Filetes de salmonete en papillote was not served at lunch. Dolores said she had been too busy helping a neighbour in trouble during the morning to do much cooking. Chickpeas, even when served in a spicy, tasty sauce, remained chickpeas.

Jaime quietly complained that helping a neighbour at the expense of a worthwhile lunch proved women were unable to get their priorities correct.

Alvarez was in bed, the soft arms of sleep about to embrace him, when the telephone rang downstairs. He ignored it.

'Enrique,' Dolores called out.

If he did not reply, she would assume he had fallen asleep and might not try to wake him . . .

'Shall I tell that man from Madrid you'll get back to him when you're out of bed?'

Only a man of Salas' nature would ring on a Saturday afternoon. He climbed out of bed, dressed, went downstairs and through to the *entrada* where the phone was on a small olive-wood table. 'Alvarez speaking, señor.'

'I am interrupting your leisure?'

'How do you mean, señor?'

'Since you are at home and not at your office. One may presume you are not working.'

'That's because I have been questioning hotel staff until very recently. I had a quick meal and was resting for a moment before returning to work.'

'I expected to hear from you before lunch.'

'It did not seem necessary to bother you since I learned nothing that was relevant.'

'A common occurrence. It seems clear that you fail to understand a negative can bear as much value as a positive.'

'When they are opposites and therefore cannot give the same answer? That is except when they are said to do so, and then how can that be correct?'

'Can you interpret what you have said?'

'When a negative is multiplied by a negative, there are those who say the result is positive. Yet if I owe ten euros and then my debt is doubled, I don't have a credit of twenty euros.'

'To explain the matter to you would take far more time than is available. How many hotels have you visited?'

'Two, señor.' Alvarez added one for luck.

'Why so few?'

'It has proven a very lengthy task. The manager was reluctant to have the staff questioned because the aparthotel was full and often the necessary staff were not immediately available.'

'You learned nothing of significance?'

'None of the staff provided any evidence to suggest one of the guests was missing.'

'And at the second hotel?'

'How d'you mean, señor?'

'You visited two hotels and have reported the results of your first enquiries. I am now asking what you learned at the second one.'

'I was momentarily a little confused.'

'Momentarily?'

'The result was again negative.'

'Then these two hotels can be dismissed from your enquiries. A clear example of how two negatives provide a positive.'

'I don't think that's much of a positive.'

'Why not?'

'If I'm trying to identify a man in a busy town and I stop someone to ask if he is Señor Fosca and he says he isn't, that's hardly a positive when there are thousands of other men who will have to be asked.'

'There are thousands of hotels and aparthotels in Llueso, Port Llueso and Playa Nueva?'

No. But—'

'Restrict your analogies to those which possess logic. Do you intend to leave home and resume your enquiries?'

'I was about to do so when you phoned.'

'You will report again tonight.'

'That is likely to be rather late, and since tomorrow is Sunday, perhaps you would prefer me to wait until Monday morning unless I am able to make a positive report rather than one which is two negatives?'

'I should prefer you to do as ordered without an inane argument. I will be at my office until well into tomorrow due to the forthcoming conference. You will not disturb my sleep.'

His own sleep had been the problem.

FIVE

Alvarez left Hotel San Deandro in Cala Roig and walked to his car. The manager had been aggressive, the staff unhelpful. The hotel boasted four stars and, he was loftily informed, no guest would ever willingly forego even a day's absence so it was unsurprising that no guest *was* absent. He had not been offered a friendly drink. Luxury could be very miserly.

He sat behind the wheel, lit a cigarette and decided to call it a night. How far could Salas expect him to widen the area of search? Mitjorn and Playa Nueva, even Cala Baston? To question the staff in all the hotels in those resorts would be an endless task. And as if that was not sufficiently disturbing, there were all the villas, chalets and flats let to tourists. Since many of these were not registered – Mallorquins had a pragmatic approach to taxes, foreigners soon learned – there were few records of which properties were let; to check if someone had disappeared and for some reason not been reported as missing, each let property would have to be identified and the owner questioned. Tomorrow, after the post-morten, it would be time to seek the aid of local newspapers.

The morgue was on the north side of the village, largely shielded by a house; lacking windows, it had the spiritless appearance of a minor supermarket. Villagers passed it on the other side of the road.

'I suppose I should comment on your prompt arrival,' Doctor Bellejos remarked with light sarcasm.

By Mallorquin standards, Alvarez was not late.

Bellejos, looking slightly theatrical, wore a white paper coat, zipper overalls, overshoes, and a hair covering. 'Since you are now here, inspector, we will begin.'

Alvarez tried, and failed, to disassociate himself from what was happening to the body on the slab of marble. Only a would-be saint wanted to be reminded what death could entail. His own doctor had recently said he should give up smoking and drink far less if he wanted to see his grandchildren. Since he wasn't married and had, to the best of his knowledge, no grandchildren, it tended to be a warning to ignore. Nevertheless, the possibility that one day he might be opened up on a marble slab . . .

'The body bears a healed scar on the neck. Do you want to see it close up?'

He didn't. Very reluctantly, he crossed and tried to view only the semicircular scar on the right of the neck, below the ear. He returned to where he had been as the photographer worked to the doctor's instructions.

Bellejos told the mortuary assistant to prepare the body, walked over to where Alvarez stood.

'I believe my colleague, who first inspected the deceased, hesitated to say if drowning was the cause of death?' Bellejos said.

'Yes.'

'He was observing the wisest forensic advice. Appearance can be both indicative and fallacious. Despite having been recovered from the bay, the deceased did not drown. Water and foreign matter entered the mouth, nostrils and throat, there were small traces in the terminal air passages, but this was not beaten into a fine froth and the lungs were not ballooned.'

'Then what killed him?'

'Laboratory tests are needed to answer that, which is why, as you saw, I have taken particular care in extracting internal samples.'

He nodded; he had not watched.

'Due to prolonged immersion in water, which is still comparatively warm, physical deterioration is such that there are no symptoms definite enough to offer an opinion other than that poisoning has to be considered.'

Yet more trouble, he thought.

He drove back to the post, went up to his office and gloomily accepted that it might be a Sunday, but although he had already worked for a long while, he might be ordered to continue. After reporting the death to the local media, he brought the bottle and a glass out of the bottom drawer in the desk, poured himself a consoling brandy. When they had spoken last night, Salas had said to phone as soon as the results of the post-mortem were known. Yet he might have forgotten. He phoned Palma, hoping, convinced, there would be no answer.

'Superior Chief Salas' office,' Ángela Torres said.

There remained the chance she was on her own. 'It's Inspector Alvarez, señorita. Can I have a word with Señor Salas?'

'He is not here.'

Relief misguided his tongue. 'Risking the pleasure of enjoying himself?'

'It will not occur to you that he has been working all morning, was recently called away and will be returning shortly.'

'I'll ring again.'

'Wait. He has just returned.'

He waited. It simply was not his day.

'Yes?'

'Inspector Alvarez, señor. I have just returned from the post-mortem.'

'Of whom?'

'I don't know.'

'It was optimistic to believe you might.'

'The victim was the man who drowned in the bay. He did not drown.'

There was a pause before Salas said: 'Are you aware there is an inconsistency in what you have just said?'

'The forensic doctor said he did not die from drowning.'

'Yet initially you referred to the victim who drowned in the bay.'

'To identify him to you, señor.'

'Have you read Alfredo Fiscá's great work, *Mutilado de hecho*, in which he wrote "fact is always a potential liar"?'

'No, señor.'

'There is little room for surprise.'

'When I referred to the dead man as having drowned, it

was to name him as the subject of the post-mortem, not to state the cause of his death.'

'In as few words as possible, ignoring any attempt to assist my understanding, what have you learned?'

'Despite all my work, I have been unable to identify the dead man. The post-mortem has established he did not die from drowning. The pathologist was reluctant to offer any cause of death, but did say it may have been poison.'

'When will the forensic results be known?'

'I have been given no estimate.'

'Perhaps you have not thought to ask for one?'

'The samples may not have yet reached the laboratory.'

'You accept that there is nothing more to be done until you have their report?'

'Far from it. I have spoken to the local papers.'

'Why?'

'To request them to publish details of the dead man in order to learn if anyone can identify him. I also spoke to the assistant director of the local news programme on the television.'

'I am at a loss to remember when you requested my permission to take such steps.'

'I reckoned the need to know his name was more urgent than observing bureaucratic rules.'

'"Bureaucratic rules", as you are pleased to call them, are designed to prevent junior officers' potential mistakes. Did you provide an adequate description of the dead man?'

'As good as I could.'

'One has to hope. It is interesting to realize that, from your point of view, a rapid response to the request would mean you would not have to question the staff in the many remaining hotels.'

'That had not occurred to me.'

'A man accused of stealing books is advised not to plead innocent because he cannot read. Have you considered the consequences if the cause of death was poisoning?'

'It is difficult at the moment to do more than accept it indicates murder, suicide or accident.'

'It is not disrespectful to the deceased to hope it was an accident and that the brief investigation into his death will not be subject to the mishaps which frequently follow one conducted by you.'

Salsa de cebollas blancas – large white onions, butter, olive oil, milk, egg yolk, marjoram, salt, and pepper – failed to dispense Alvarez's sense of grievance. 'The superior chief would complain about how an angel flies.' He helped himself to more wine, but not sufficient, since Dolores had been regarding him as he did so.

'In trouble yet again?' Jaime was annoyed that Dolores looked at him as he was about to pick up the bottle.

'He condemned me for using my initiative.'

Having cleared the table and set down on it almonds, oranges and bananas, Dolores sat, picked up a baked almond. 'Why did he behave like that?' She put the almond in her mouth.

'We can't identify the man who drowned in the bay. I've been working day and night to find out who he was and have failed, so I got in touch with the papers and local TV, request them to publicize his description and ask if someone can put a name to him. How could one show better initiative than that? Yet Salas blasts me for not obtaining his permission to act. Only a man like him bothers about rules.'

'He is a Madrileño, which is why he thinks he need show no manners when he phones here and demands to know where you are. Even a peasant first wishes a good morning.'

'When it's the afternoon?' Jaime asked.

'You have already drunk too well?'

'Haven't had the chance,' he muttered.

Not a word of commiseration from either of them. It had, Alvarez decided, become an age in which compassion was forgotten. He watched Dolores go into the kitchen to get him a steel knife to peel an orange.

On Thursday, the sky was heavily overcast, the rain was light but steady, the wind was cool. Tourists were reminded that only in travel posters was the sun always shining.

Alvarez had to park well away from the post. He walked through the damp streets, dully answered the duty guard's welcome, went up to his office and sat behind the desk. The phone rang. Salas asking him why he had ignored yet another nonsensical bureaucratic rule? The bank manager suggesting he might like to have a word about his overdraft? Dolores telling him she was lunching with a friend and he could prepare his own meal? He lifted the receiver.

'Roberto here, Enrique. Thought you'd want to know they've brought in four more bodies from the bay.'

'What!'

'Naked, so no ID again.'

'What the hell's going on? This'll make life impossible.'

'One man lost his arm, hacked off; the only woman is headless. The doc says they've been floating around for six months or more.'

Common sense replaced Alvarez's panic. 'You bastard!'

Plá laughed.

'I've a good mind to arrest you for wasting the police's time.'

'Can't waste something of no value.'

Alvarez replaced the receiver. Plá's sense of humour was juvenile. The phone rang again. He picked up the receiver. 'I know. A shipload of elephants are swimming in the bay.'

'I beg your pardon, Inspector Alvarez,' Ángela Torres said, her tone expressing contempt.

'I thought . . . that you . . . Well, because he had just . . .'

'One moment.'

'Are you in the transport business?' Salas asked.

'No, señor.'

'Then why are you expecting a shipload of elephants?'

'I'm not.'

'You frequently expect what you are not expecting?'

'I thought Señorita Torres was a friend.'

'Is he expecting elephants?'

'No.'

'Have such animals had a major influence in your past life?'

'No.'

'I may have previously mentioned I have a friend who is an internationally recognized psychologist. Since I first described you to him, he has taken considerable interest in your career. Your behaviour regarding elephants may well be of value to him.'

'I can explain, señor.'

'Do so to him. I find no benefit in trying to comprehend the incomprehensible.'

'But can one comprehend the incomprehensible?'

'You are well advised not to consider matters which are beyond you. Have you spoken to the forensic laboratory regarding the dead man?'

'They can't tell us anything yet.'

'Inform me when they can, and do so without reference to elephants.'

Alvarez replaced the receiver. A moment later, it rang. He was about to be forbidden to mention tigers?

'Enrique? I—'

'Who's that?'

'Rafael Nadal inviting you to a game of tennis.'

'You've just landed me in a load of trouble.'

'You have been out of it?'

'Thanks to you, I told the superior chief I was expecting a shipload of elephants.'

'From you, he shouldn't have found that odd. I've had a chat with a neat little number, blonde, cunningly upholstered . . .'

'Not interested.'

'Then I won't bother. After all, she was only saying she may know who the missing man could be.'

'Why, who, when?'

'You're not interested.'

'Do you want Traffic to accuse you of dangerous driving and take your car for crushing?'

'You bring a new meaning to friendship.'

'Who is she?'

'Works for Nirvana Holidays, an English company which does downmarket package holidays for people wanting to stay in a villa. In the middle of September, a man on his own – Colin Kerr – arrived for a month's stay in one of the cheapest villas.'

'Unusual, renting a villa for that long when on his own.'

'Reckoned to find company here. And he said he'd come to meet friends. About halfway through the tenancy, Anna read in *Ultima Hora* that the dead man from the bay had a semicircular scar on his neck. This reminded her of Colin Kerr, who seemed to have temporarily absented his letting. She wondered if he could be the dead man.'

'Friends would have reported him missing.'

'I didn't like to contradict her, just thanked her very much for getting in touch and said it was not everyone who'd have bothered.'

'If you were polite, you were trying your hand, even though you were on duty.'

'Can't expect you to appreciate courtesy.'

They said goodbye. Should he report to Salas? Alvarez asked himself. On the one hand, it would show how sharply on the ball he was; on the other, since Kerr might well be staying with friends and saw no reason to acquaint the company's office of the fact, Salas would want to know whether he had spoken to the friends and then would demand he worked twenty-five hours a day until he identified them.

He looked at his watch. Not long before he could reasonably return home. Better to wait and consider what he had learned than rush down to the port to question the woman.

Would a man book a month's stay in a villa when he might be unlucky and have to spend the whole time on his own? He would not do his own cooking and to eat out for every meal would be expensive, yet his choice of a downmarket villa suggested his funds were low. Yet good friends would surely have alerted the authorities had their guest gone missing.

Anna might be able to provide some answers. How had Rafael described her? A neat little number.

SIX

Ángela Torres rang at a quarter past nine the next morning as Alvarez entered his office and congratulated himself on his nearly-on-time arrival.

'I have been asked by the superior chief to question whether your examination of airline passengers' lists from the island have revealed any discrepancies.'

The question momentarily perplexed him.

'Did any passenger not take a flight for which he was booked?'

'I have found no such absence, señorita.'

She did not say goodbye, but her manners were fashioned by Salas.

Alvarez drummed on the desk with his fingers. He had spoken the truth. He had discovered no such discrepancy since he had not thought to do so. He stopped drumming, stood. In view of her question, Salas might soon be phoning, and it would be in his interest to spend at least part of the morning away from the office.

The office of Nirvana Holidays was in a road which ran down to the bay. Since its main aim was to assist clients when it was unavoidable, the furnishing was of a plebeian nature. Anna sat behind a right-angled working surface on which were phone, computer, printer and company brochures. Plá had been grudging in his description of her. She had a face and form to launch any number of ships.

'You want something?' she asked in rough Mallorquin, identifying him as a local from his dress and manner.

'I'd like to ask you one or two things.'

'I'm busy,' she said in Castilian, making it clear that even if she were not busy, she would not welcome his company. Age – not that he was near becoming aged – gained far less respect, along with authority, than it once had.

'Inspector Alvarez, Cuerpo General de Policía.'

She regarded him more closely. 'Surprising.'

An implied criticism?

'I suppose you're here because of Señor Kerr. You're wasting your time since I told the other bloke all I know.'

'He was Policía.'

'What's that matter?'

About to explain, he noted her mocking amusement. Perhaps she thought she knew where his thoughts had wandered. Even a hatchet-faced harridan could imagine a man looked at her with desire. 'You informed the Policía that Señor Kerr, a client of yours, had a scar on his neck which made you think he might be the dead man.'

'So?'

'Will you describe the scar?'

'I did to the other chap.'

'I'm sorry to ask you to repeat yourself, but I would be grateful if you would tell me now.' Members of the Cuerpo were expected to be polite, and there were times when to do so might prove an advantage. 'Whereabouts was it?'

'Right side of the neck under the ear.'

'The shape and size?'

'Kind of half circular, and maybe eight centimetres long.'

'And he seems to be missing?'

'Yes.'

'Is his villa locked?'

'It's now been let to the next tenants.'

'What about any contents that were left?'

'Packed.'

'In the circumstances, I think it might have been advisable to have informed the authorities . . .'

'I told the boss.'

He smiled. 'Not exactly authority.'

'Try working for him and find out.'

'I meant the Policía or the Cuerpo.'

'When it just looked like he'd found a companion and gone walking?'

'You think that's likely?'

'Booked in and asked me out for a meal in one breath.'

'Where did you eat?'

'You think you're amusing? I told him to get lost. Is there anything more or can I get on with my work?'

'You have what came out of his villa?'

'It's in a box in the safe.'

'Is it full of diamonds?'

'Four thousand two hundred euros.'

He was alarmed as well as surprised. The case was becoming ever more complicated with the possible identification. 'In cash?'

'And every note is still in the box.'

'I'd never doubt that.'

'First thing you'd wonder would be how much has been pinched.'

'You misjudge me.'

'I doubt it.'

'I need to see the box.'

'You can count up to four thousand?'

She went in to an inner room, returned with a medium-sized cardboard box which she put down on the desk. 'You'll need to sign for it.'

'Then perhaps you'll be kind enough to make out some kind of form?'

She worked quickly at the keyboard, checked the screen, activated the printer, passed him a sheet of paper. He wrote 'Contents unchecked' before he signed.

She read what he had written. 'You lot would suspect your own shadows.'

'Nothing personal, I assure you. Rules and regulations.' He thanked her for her assistance, returned to his car, put the box on the back seat. Settled behind the wheel, he stared through the windscreen and watched two young women, in bikinis, as they walked away from the communal swimming pool.

He drove to Llueso and the post, carried the box up to his office. He cleared the top of the desk with a sweep of the hand, opened the box. The clothes suggested Kerr had not expected changeable weather and had had to buy a Spanish-made roll-neck sweater. An unopened bottle of Glenfiddich bore the paper seal to show duty had been paid in Spain. In two padded envelopes were forty-two hundred-euro notes. In a battered cigarette case were six spliffs, their nature confirmed by smelling. There was a small notebook. Kerr had noted times of departure from Stansted and flight number; the same for Palma; the address of Nirvana Holidays in Port Llueso; and an address: Son Dragó, Roca Nesca, in the port.

A man who went on a package holiday and rented a down-market villa was someone who did not have much money. Yet he had bought an expensive sweater, malt whisky, and had forty-two thousand euros in cash.

He would have to speak to Salas. After lunch.

It was late afternoon.

'Señor, I have been informed of a tenant in a rented villa who appears to have disappeared. His name is Colin Kerr. I have examined the contents he left in the villa and they are of interest because of the contradictions they present. I am confident I have identified the dead man.'

'Your reasons for so firm a conclusion?'

'I was informed that Señorita Berjón, who works for a villa letting agency, had read a report in a local newspaper concerning the missing man; she had reason to believe she might know who he was. I have spoken to her, and she gave me the name of Kerr.'

'Why was I not informed?'

'I am informing you now, señor.'

'Clearly, some considerable time after you had reason to believe she might be able to provide important information.'

'I thought it better to question her first in case it proved to be a false alarm.'

'There was reason for the possible identification to cause you alarm?'

'No, but—'

'Then you should choose your words more carefully.'

'It seemed better to check she was correct before I reported to you so I would know I was not talking nonsense.'

'I find your acceptance of that possibility refreshing. You have shown her a photograph of the dead man?'

'No.'

'Why not?'

'His appearance might well have shocked her.'

'Explain why you are ready to accept her identification while failing to gain visual confirmation. Did this woman provide any facts to support her claim?'

'Kerr's absence from the villa and leaving his possessions behind. When I asked if he bore any noticeable physical features, she named a scar. Her description of that very closely matched the actual scar on the dead man.'

'You will show her a photograph of the scar for final confirmation.'

'Very well, señor, but it is to be hoped she does not have hysterics.'

'Cold water will very soon bring them to a stop. Why did you refer to contradictions?'

'Kerr travelled on a cheap package holiday which must mean he was not heavy with cash.'

'One is either well off or not well off; one is not heavy with cash.'

'Unless one's robbed a bank?'

'As I have said before, humour is not your métier.'

'Despite being not well off, in his possession was a locally bought, expensive sweater, a locally bought bottle of malt whisky and four thousand two hundred euros in one hundred euro notes. In addition, there were six spliffs.'

'Have these facts led you to any possible conclusion?'

'Because of the money, he may be in the drug or money laundering trade.'

'Have you learned anything more which gives weight to either possibility?'

'I'm not certain.'

'Why not?

'There was a notebook. In it was an address in Port Llueso. Why would Kerr have noted a personal address?'

'You have not considered that he might have friends on the island?'

'The address was Son Dragó, Roca Nesca.'

'Have you thought to determine who lives there?'

'Señor Ashton, until he died very recently.'

'You are prepared to accept he might have had some criminal connection with the dead man?'

'It's indicative Kerr should have that address . . .'

'I should not expect you to appreciate the character of an English gentleman. I met Señor Ashton at a party he gave to aid charity, and he would have had no part in anything of a criminal or even morally doubtful nature.'

'But . . . Señor, according to a book I have just read, English gentlemen are not as gentlemanly as we believe. It's not all that long since the owner of a mansion who invited guests to stay with him had their names put up on bedroom doors. This prevented male guests who wandered during the night disturbing the wrong lady.'

'The nature of the books you read provides a lens into your character and explains how you could consider the impossible.'

'I wondered if I should speak to his wife, though she will still be in mourning. I would do so very diplomatically.'

'The devil smiles at man's mistaken pride. You will not question Señora Ashton until there is much greater and reasonable cause for doing so.'

Alvarez walked into the office of Nirvana Holidays. Anna was speaking to a client, trying to explain that if he had left his driving licence in England, the hire-car firm in Port Llueso could not allow him to have a car. There was no point in her speaking on his behalf to the Policía, the Guardia, or the British Consul.

Before the client left, he expressed his opinion of her behaviour when the firm's brochure had offered expert aid to any client who needed help.

'Do you often get them like that?' Alvarez asked.

'Every day. What do you want this time?'

'To show you a photograph.'

'Of you winning the over-sixties marathon?'

'I'll need to wait thirty-five years before I do that.'

'You need to look in a mirror.'

He brought the photograph out of a large envelope. 'It's of the dead man, but only shows the scar so you don't need to worry.'

'You think I'm the fainting type?' she asked as she took the photograph.

'Do you identify the scar as similar to the one on Kerr's neck? As soon as I have an answer, we'll go to the nearest café and you can enjoy a restorative.'

She briefly studied the photo. 'That's him.'

'Can you be certain?'

'Yes.'

'Good.' He took the photograph back, returned it to the envelope. 'So, let's restore.'

'D'you mind waiting until I phone my fiancé to ask him to join us?'

'I'm sorry. If I'd known . . . But you're not wearing a ring.'

'The Hope diamond is being recut.'

Back in his car, he lowered the sunshade and studied his face in the small mirror on the back. Old enough to run in an over-sixties marathon? She was a bitch.

SEVEN

Alvarez crossed the old square, went into Club Llueso and the bar, stared at the bottles on the shelves as his mind drifted.

Behind the bar, Roca moved and stood in front of him. 'Have you had a heavy night, even by your own standards?'

'Why ask?'

'Because you haven't rudely shouted for a coñac.'

'It's work.'

'Disturbingly unfamiliar?'

'My superior asks the impossible.'

'Don't they all? So are you ordering or d'you want to pay a parking fee?'

'A coñac.'

'Ever heard of that little word "please"?'

'Not in here.'

Alvarez carried a well-filled glass over to a window seat. Bitter thoughts were briefly banished when he saw a young brunette whose frock appeared to caress her as she walked towards the steps up to the old square. *She* would never confuse him with being in his mid-sixties.

He drank. Salas, unwilling to accept the worth of those under his command, had vetoed the questioning of Señora Ashton. But he had not mentioned the staff at Son Dragó. One of them might be able to understand if there was any significance in the address being in Kerr's notebook. And there was pleasure to be gained in uncovering evidence which would prove Salas had made a stupid decision . . . Yet was so ephemeral a pleasure worth the effort?

His glass was empty, and he took it to the bar to be refilled.

Dolores said: 'You are troubled, Enrique?'

'I'm trying to decide whether or not to follow up an idea,' Alvarez replied.

'Was she telling you to get lost or giving you the catch-me-if-you-can routine?' Jaime queried.

Her tone became sharp. 'As my mother used to say, a man's mind is always searching.' She spoke to Alvarez. 'The problem is with work?'

'If I take one course of action, I may gain the chance to prove to Salas he's been wrong.'

'There is a preferable alternative?'

'No, but it would mean having to undertake a hell of a lot of extra work.'

'Without doubt, for you a problem without a solution.' She stood. 'There is one decision you will take now.'

'What?'

'To help clear the table.'

He watched her carry plates through to the kitchen. Women had never been good philosophers, since their thoughts never rose above a domestic level.

He braked to a halt in front of Son Dragó, stepped out of the car into the sunshine. He looked across blue Llueso Bay, with its mountainous backing; at s'Albufereta de Llueso, now a nature reserve; at Port Llueso, saved from overdevelopment by those few who placed charm above profit; at the final thrust of the Serra de Tramuntana which reached eastwards to the lighthouse at Cap de Parelona and on which ran a road of endless, vertiginous twists and turns, bordered by plunging rock faces. A road to terrify someone who, as did he, suffered from altophobia.

In the long area that ran from road to house and from house to the end of the promontory grew, in no planned form, indigenous plants, or those which over very many years, sometimes since the time of the Moors, had become so. For him, a far more attractive sight than the multicoloured, highly cultivated plants in the gardens of most foreign owned properties. The palm trees appeared to have escaped the bug which was killing so many. Saved by the enveloping sea? In the spring, the many almond trees would provide clouds of white. Had he been a god, he would live here, not on Olympus.

He heard footsteps and turned, faced a squarely built man

with a face sketched by sun, wind, and rain, dressed in working clothes.

'Thought it must be you, seeing as you'd nothing to do but stand and stare.'

'Felipe Salcedo!'

'Felipe García.'

'Of course. But as they say, call a rose a bramble and it will still smell sweet. What are you doing here?'

'With a mattock in me hand, you need telling?'

'I thought you were in building.'

'So I was, even after I bloody near fell head first down the well we were deepening. But a foreigner cleared off leaving all the bills unpaid for a new house, the boss retired, and it was time to find a new firm. Only, work had become tighter than a Mestarian's pocket because of those sods in banks, and the old woman was bellyaching because I didn't bring home good money and still spent time in a bar.'

'Women dislike bars.'

'Dislike anything what gives a man a bit of fun.'

'Had you previously done any garden work?'

'No.'

'How did you persuade the señor to take you on?'

'Told him I wasn't no pansy gardener, but the stuff he wanted looking after, I'd known since I was a kid.'

'It's an unusual garden.'

'It's what he liked. Growing island history, he called it. Waste of money, a mate of mine says. If some plants are dying out, let 'em, there's plenty more. The señor wanted to conserve. See that tree?'

Alvarez looked at a very ordinary, spindly tree with dull green leaves.

'He said there wasn't more than a dozen of them left and they only grow on the island.'

'Don't recognize it. What's it called?'

'Can't remember. Some Latin name which sounds like you're gargling.'

'Can't be much you haven't got?'

'There's palms, olives, oaks, carobs, almonds, lentiscs, mastics, pistachios, strawberry trees, heathers, buckthorns,

myrtles, what he called the sacred tree of Venus, whoever she
is, and a lot more.'

'How did the señor regard your gardening skills?'

'He told me more than once that it was just how he wanted
things. And the señorita said as how, shortly before he died,
she had to wheel him over to a window so as he could look
out at everything.'

'It was kind of her to tell you that.'

'Came natural to her. Like when Juana was really ill.'

'Your wife?'

'Daughter. Doctor didn't know what was wrong. The señora
said Juana was to go into a *clinica*, and they saved her. Ain't
many, however rich, what would have paid the bills they did
for an employee's child.'

'You sound as if you have a great respect for her.'

'Surprises you?'

'D'you think she'll inherit the estate?'

'Why shouldn't she?'

'Rich men can act strangely. A billionaire in America died
not long back and left his children nothing because he reckoned they should make their own way through life, same as
he had to.'

'Silly bugger.'

'Did he get on well with the señora?'

'Married to her, wasn't he?'

'Doesn't mean everything was sweet.'

'You've a miserable mind.'

'Comes from the job.'

'Find another one.'

'Perhaps I should try gardening.'

'When you look like you haven't the strength to pull out a
bramble?'

'Someone said the señor was keen on sailing.'

'Often went out in his yacht.'

'With the señora?'

'If he wasn't going far. She told me she enjoyed it for a
while, but not when it went on day after day and all you saw
was the sea.'

'Did he sail far?'

'Menorca, Ibiza, France, Italy, Turkey, Morocco.'

'Did you ever go on the boat with him?'

'When he was having trouble with the motor.'

'Thought it was a sailing yacht.'

'Never heard of being trapped on a lee shore?'

'Have you?'

'He told me about it.'

'Now tell me.'

'A tide or a wind takes you in towards the shore and you can't put up enough sail to escape. Without an engine, you smash on to the rocks and likely drown.'

'I'll stick to land. When the engine seemed to be uneasy, you were out with him if it needed to be put right?'

'Weren't to haul the ropes.'

'You're an engineer as well as a gardener and builder?'

'I know enough about engines to get it going again.'

'Did you ever go to Morocco with him?'

'No.'

'How often did he sail there?'

'As often as he wanted.'

'Did the señora go with him?'

'Ain't I said, she didn't like long trips?'

'Did he bring stuff back from there?'

'You want to charge him duty?'

'Not my problem. What kind of things did he bring?'

'Herbs, spices, stuff like that and some kind of prepared food. Gave me and the wife some of that. She tried it and chucked it.'

'Nothing else?'

'Copper caskets. Collected 'em.'

'Antiques?'

'Might have been. Messed around in what he said was classical decoration. Some of them came from hundreds of years back.'

'What sort of size?'

'Thirty, fifty centimetres long.'

'Were they heavy?'

'Copper ain't made of feathers.'

'The weight might have been what was in them?'

García shrugged his shoulders.

'You never saw what was inside?'

'Don't poke me nose where it's not wanted. Why are you going on about them?'

'I'm interested in old things.'

'Kind of family feeling?'

'I want to know—'

'I've finished with answering.'

'You want another feather in your cap from hindering the law? Builder, gardener, mechanic, criminal?'

'You're a daft sod.'

'D'you get strangers wandering around the estate?'

'On the two days when they're open to the public it's like Palma. Leave enough mess and damage for twice as many. But the señor takes a couple of euros from all of them and gives it to charity.'

'What about people at other times?'

'Because the garden's mentioned in guidebooks, there's some who think the place is public.'

'Have you—'

'I was mentioned in one of them,' García proudly interrupted.

'Favourably?'

'Said I was a real expert gardener.'

'Fame indeed! You've heard about the body fished out of the bay?'

'I can read.'

'He had the name Roca Nesca written down in his notebook. So you could have seen him wandering around. Five, six centimetres taller than you, slim, wavy brown hair, kind of rat-faced good-looking, white skin because he hadn't seen the sun for a time, a very noticeable scar on his neck. Maybe he was in the garden, hoping to ask your advice.'

'Ain't seen anyone like that.'

'Who works in the house?'

'What's it to you?'

'I'll have to ask them questions similar to those I've asked you, and it's polite to know their names.'

'Same as you knew mine?'

'Is there a big staff?'

'The señor didn't like too many people around. He'd often come out here and sit in the shade, not doing anything but enjoying what was around him. Said the greatest luxury was peace and quiet.'

'Tell me the names of the staff.'

'Manuel, Beatriz, Inés, and a couple who come on alternative days to help clean.'

'Manuel who?'

'Benavides. Comes from Valladolid. Calls himself the butler.' García hawked and spat an unspoken comment on social delusions.

'And Beatriz?'

'Does the cooking.'

'Is she good at it?'

'The señor liked his grub so he wouldn't have had her if she weren't. Not that I've ever said to the wife how good she is. Nothing starts a cat-row faster than telling a wife she ain't the sharpest cook.'

'How right you are! I ought to move.'

'Don't reckon to stop you.'

Alvarez walked slowly. A pattern was beginning to emerge. He went around the house to the back door and, since this was 'Mallorquin territory', did not bother to knock, but opened it and entered a small square, off which were three inner doors. He called out. Benavides entered, was momentarily surprised to see him.

Alvarez introduced himself. 'I've come to have a word with you. It's been a tiring day, so is there somewhere we can sit?'

'If you will kindly follow me, inspector, we will go into the staff sitting-room.'

They walked along a corridor, past the kitchen from which came evocative culinary scents, turned into a small room, reasonably furnished.

'Please sit where you would like.'

Alvarez was disturbed by Benavides' obsequious manner, but accepted that someone from Valladolid could not be expected to enjoy the same sense of equality as a Mallorquin. 'I'm hoping you will be able to help me over one or two matters.'

'If that is possible, I shall be happy to do so.'

'I need to find out more about Kerr, the man who drowned in the bay. You'll have read or heard he had a noticeable scar on his neck below the right ear and this was large enough to make for easy identification. Did he come here before he died?'

'Had he done so, inspector, in view of all the publicity, I would have immediately reported the matter.'

'It's heartening to hear that.' And unusual. The islanders would denounce each other without hesitation, but saw little need to inform the police about something which did not concern themselves. 'I've looked through the possessions of the dead man, left in the villa he was renting, and amongst them was a notebook in which was written this address. I had a word with Felipe before coming to the house and asked if he'd seen someone resembling Colin Kerr wandering about the estate. He hadn't. So I thought Kerr might have come directly to the house. You tell me he didn't. To your knowledge, was Kerr a friend or acquaintance of the señor?'

'I have no reason to believe so.'

'He never called at the house?'

'Again, I fear I cannot help you.'

'Then likely Felipe was right.'

'In what respect?'

'Kerr probably read about the gardens in a travel guide, made a note to look at them, never did so.'

'That sounds reasonable.'

'I'd better have a word with Inés and Beatriz now, to make certain I've spoken to everyone.'

'I can assure you they will agree with what I have said.'

'My boss will cast doubts on anything not told directly to me; there are times when he finds reason even to doubt what I say.'

'You have an unfortunate superior?'

'Doesn't everyone?'

'Those of us lucky enough to work here would disagree.'

'D'you know who'll inherit the estate?'

'No. But it is the wish of us all that Señora Ashton does.'

'She couldn't enjoy a better recommendation.'

'An opinion, inspector. An employee does not recommend.'

'Not even to a would-be employee?'

Benavides managed a cramped, brief smile.

'Did the señor and señora get on well together?'

'Yes.'

'Roca Nesca promotes perfect relationships.'

'Marriage, in their case.'

'Even a marriage made in heaven has its downsides. They could hardly be human and not have had a row or two.'

'If that had been the case, the discussion would have been in private. The señor always behaved as a man in his position is expected to.'

'You never heard so much as a spat?'

'The señora would sometimes disagree with him, but she always expressed herself in a gentlewomanly manner.'

'A marriage not only made in heaven, but spent there.'

'You will excuse my saying that it is a shame to disparage the happiness of others.'

'It was awe, not disparagement. When the señora did quietly express her opinion, what was it likely to be about?'

'Domestic matters.'

'Who was likely to win?'

'They would come to a happy agreement. Indeed, I can recall only the one instance in which one might say it was obvious they strongly disagreed.'

'Tell me about it.'

'The señor had to return to England for three weeks, and since he would be in Manchester, said they'd travel together and she could visit her old friends. She did not wish to go, and that upset the señor.'

'She had a reason for staying here?'

'I cannot answer.'

'A young, male friend?'

Benavides' tone became very butlerish. 'She has friends, all of whom remained just friends.'

'No honey buttering?'

'I do not understand.'

'Secret smiles, furtive touches.'

'You completely mistake the señora.'

'No young male friends ever stay here?'

'I can recall only Señor Browyer, and it may disappoint you to know that neither the señor nor the señora enjoyed his company.'

'Then what was his attraction?'

'He was a nephew of the señor.'

'And what was wrong with him?'

'It is not my place to comment.'

'Move on until it is.'

'The señor was of a generous nature, yet I inadvertently heard him say to the señora that he had more than once lent money to Señor Browyer, none of which had been repaid, so he was not going to lend him any more.'

'Browyer is a sponger?'

Benavides did not answer.

'Where does he live?'

'In England.'

'When did he last stay here?'

'In May.'

'There has been no word from him since then?'

'I cannot be certain.'

'Why not?'

'I answered the phone not long before the señor died. The caller asked to speak to the señor. I answered that he was not at home and asked the caller for his name. He rang off. His voice had been muffled, but it reminded me of Señor Browyer's. I did not express the possibility to the señor, but I did later hear him speaking very angrily on the telephone when there was another call from the same man.'

'Browyer asking for more money?'

'I cannot answer.'

'And you've no idea where the call came from?'

'When I answered, I could just hear a voice speaking Mallorquin in the background.'

'If it was Browyer, he was phoning from somewhere on the island?'

'It would seem very likely.'

'Is there anything more you can tell me?'

'I think not.'

'Thank you for your help. And will you ask Inés to come along and have a word?'

'Inspector, permit me to say that she is young for her age and of a simple nature due to the conditions under which she lives. She will be very worried and probably frightened by you questioning her.'

'Why are you telling me this?'

'I hope it might persuade you to allow me to be here while you speak to her, then she will not become scared.'

'I prefer her to be on her own.'

'Then . . . if she is very nervous and becomes confused, perhaps you will understand?'

'I am used to confusion. And if it'll make you less worried, I question *any* young woman with restraint.'

Alvarez watched Benavides, clearly less than happy, leave. Perhaps he doubted an inspector could speak to anyone, young or old, with restraint.

There was a knock on the door. He called out and Inés entered, clearly nervous and uneasy. He thanked her for coming and assured her he would be as brief as possible; if she became upset, she should tell him and they'd have a break. 'You know why I'm here?'

She nodded as she stared down at the floor.

'I have to find out why the unfortunate man drowned. Of course, you've no idea why he was swimming in the bay, so all I have to ask is if, before then, you ever saw a man with a large scar on his neck who came to the house?'

She looked quickly at him, then back at the floor.

He waited before he said: 'Can you remember if you did?'

She said nothing.

He stood, crossed to the door, now watched by her, opened it and called out. Benavides quickly appeared. Alvarez explained the problem and asked Benavides to return with him.

Benavides spoke to her quietly in a tone which contained no hint of butlership.

She said: 'I only . . .' then stopped.

'Inés, inspector, only opens the front door to a caller if I am unavailable and Beatriz is too busy in the kitchen to leave it.'

'And she has not done so and faced a man with a scar?'

'Have you?' Benavides asked her.

She shook her head.

'Then we don't need to bother you any more, Inés,' Alvarez said.

She hurried out of the room, and Benavides began to follow her until stopped.

'Will you ask Beatriz to come along?' Alvarez said.

'I think she will be very reluctant to do so, inspector.'

'Why?'

'I understand the señora has eaten so little recently that Beatriz is cooking her favourite dish in the hope it will tempt her. Beatriz will want it to be perfect, and any interruption might prevent this.'

'What's the dish?'

'*Oblades amb bolets.*'

'I'm not prepared to take the risk of spoiling that. I'll speak to her at some other time.'

'I will tell her.'

'Do you get a chance to have a taste?'

'The señora said we were always to eat the same as she and the señor did.'

'You must be enjoying haute cuisine!'

As he drove away, Alvarez wondered if there was an à la carte or a fixed menu in heaven? *Oblades amb bolets.* Turbot, mushrooms, onion, olive oil, white wine, lemon, parsley, fennel, salt, pepper . . . Surely they would serve that, since the dish must have originated in heaven.

'Yes?' Ángela Torres asked, for some reason less sharpishly than usual.

'Inspector Alvarez speaking. Is the superior chief there?'

'No.'

'Will you tell him I have spoken to the staff at Son Dragó, with the exception of the cook, and they testify Kerr did not call at the house, nor was he seen in the gardens.'

'Is that all?'

'I think so.'

She did not say goodbye; he had not expected her to. He checked the time, decided it should be all right to leave the office in ten minutes. The phone rang. He swore as he lifted the receiver. 'Inspector Alvarez . . .'

'What the devil are you doing, disobeying my orders?' Salas asked.

'I have not disobeyed them, señor.'

'You have just informed my secretary that you spoke to the staff at Son Dragó.'

'To Benavides and Inés . . .'

'You would like to explain why that was not flagrant disobedience?'

'You forbade me to speak to Señora Ashton, for a reason you did not state . . .'

'Nothing could have been clearer.'

'You did not say I must not question the staff.'

'Because I forgot you were incapable of understanding a negative is not an indirect positive.'

'If it were, mathematics as we know it would be upset.'

'A subject which at present is not of the slightest relevance and of which you are likely to have little knowledge.'

'I was thinking of the supposition that two negatives make a positive.'

'It is fact, not a supposition.'

'That I do not understand what I am not to do, means I must understand even when I don't?'

'It doesn't need a double negative to cause you to ignore the simplest instruction. Have you interviewed all the staff?'

'As I informed Señorita Torres, not yet.'

'Why not?'

'Beatriz was cooking, and had I interrupted her, this might easily have ruined a golden dish.'

'Was the intended consumer Midas?'

'I don't think there was anyone but the señora.'

'Can you give a valid reason for not questioning a witness solely because she was cooking?'

'But it was *Oblades amb bolets*.'

'You fail to understand it matters not a damn if it was dried cod?'

'It would to the señora.'

'You will question the cook this afternoon, whatever she is

doing, and report immediately. You will not excuse failure on the grounds she was preparing the golden calf. You understand?'

'Yes, señor. I have learned something interesting.'

'By your judgement?'

'The señor's nephew, Browyer, visited Son Dragó more than once. He kept bumming the señor for money.'

'It pleases you to use the language of an indigent peon? Explain why it is significant.'

'The señor finally had had enough of Browyer's "borrowing" and refused to give him a cent more. There was a row, and it seems Browyer didn't visit the house again, yet very shortly before the señor died, there was a phone call from a man who wouldn't name himself, but whom Benavides judged to be Browyer even though he was trying to disguise his voice. That this was so was borne out when Benavides heard Mallorquin spoken in the background. The call made the señor angry.'

'Did you describe the information as interesting?'

'As you have often said, señor, money is the prime motive for crime.'

'Need I remind you that Señor Ashton died from natural causes and it is Kerr's death you are investigating?'

'I could not be that remiss.'

'You overrate the unlikelihood.'

'There must be a connection.'

'You will suggest what that is?'

'I haven't yet checked with hotels to find out if he is a guest in one of them, but—'

'I shouldn't expect you to act with such celerity.'

'It's all a question of time, señor. As possibly the only surviving relative of Señor Ashton, it's possible Browyer is due to inherit a large sum of money.'

'Possible is a word of evasion. Presumably, you have not yet bothered to determine the contents of the señor's will?'

'No, because of everything that's going on.'

'An expression which leaves ample room for inefficiency. I will not trouble you to try to explain what is more important than to know the contents.'

'I reckon we face three possibilities.'

'Name them.'

'Kerr had information which would cause Señor Ashton to disinherit Browyer; Browyer owed the señor so much money, only the latter's death could leave him solvent; Browyer learned about the smuggling and the profits that made and decided to take it over.'

'You have provided only three, not six, impossible suggestions.'

'I am convinced there is a connection between the two deaths.'

'You have questioned Browyer?'

'Not yet.'

'Your conviction was not sufficient to suggest it was important to do so?'

'I don't know where he is staying if he's still on the island.'

'It would help solve the problem by questioning hotel staff.'

'That would take—'

'You were about to suggest it would entail considerable work on your part?'

'That would not be of any account if I learned where he was and he could help us.'

'You will no doubt be grateful it may no longer be necessary to go to such trouble.'

'But just a list of the hotels and—'

'Such a list, including aparthotels and villas to let, with the names of the current occupants, is being installed in Spain and should now be available on this island.'

'I'll check that out immediately, señor.'

EIGHT

Banks were closed on Saturdays, their concern being with the staff, not clients. On Monday, Alvarez walked into the small vestibule of Banco Llueso in which were two ATMs, entered through the main area and into the manager's office.

'You have an appointment?' Pagés spoke sharply. His was a frustrating life. Many of the customers were wealthy, a few were rich, but he was in a strained financial position since he had an extravagant wife and four children.

'Inspector Alvarez, Cuerpo.'

'What is the trouble?' He foresaw trouble with ease.

'I doubt it means any for you.'

He seldom trusted another man's judgement; faulty optimism was widespread.

'D'you mind if I sit? It's tiring weather with unusual heat and humidity for the time of year.'

'Statistics show that over a twenty-year period, it is not unusual.'

Alvarez, accepting he wasn't going to be asked to sit, sat. 'Statistics remind me I read recently there are many fewer five-hundred notes in circulation than a year ago.'

'They are not popular.'

'Not with the holder of one?'

'You have reason for speaking to me?'

'I'm investigating the death of Colin Kerr, the man who died in the bay and whose identity we have only just determined.'

'How does his death give you cause to be here?'

'Indirectly. First, I need to confirm the late Señor Ashton had one or more accounts with you.'

'With the bank for whom I work.'

'Then did he make any large withdrawals in cash during the last six months?'

'You have an authorization for being given this information?'

'I thought we could avoid all the trouble that sort of thing causes. And Señora Ashton will not object to my knowing.'

'As I understand from your unusual request, you would like me to give details of the late señor's account, even though, by law, it is now under the aegis of the state until probation is granted.'

'I'm not trying to alter anything . . .'

'You will require the necessary authorization before I may provide any information.'

'There would be no need for me to mention how I obtained it . . .'

'I must express my great surprise that a member of the Cuerpo should seek to subvert the law.'

'All I'm trying to do is save both of us unnecessary trouble.'

'The road from improbity to perfidy is short. If you have nothing more to say, inspector, you may leave.'

Pagés had no idea how and why the world continued to turn rather than grind to a halt. Irritation led Alvarez to a nearby bar.

'Señor,' Alvarez said over the phone, 'I need an authorization addressed to Señor Pagés, Banco Llueso, to allow me to examine Señor Ashton's accounts.'

'Why do you require to do that?' Salas asked.

'The manager is so wedded to conformity, he isn't willing to slip me the figure I need.'

'It is always difficult to understand what you are attempting to say. Salvaging what is available in your jumble of illogical words – a man can only be wedded to another human – it would seem you have asked the manager to provide information which he is forbidden to do without legal authorization. Have I translated correctly?'

'It would have saved everyone trouble.'

'One incurs, not saves, trouble by ignoring the rules.'

'It would save in this case.'

'A rule is to be observed, not bypassed, especially by those whose duty it is to uphold the law.'

'Señor, I have every regard for the law; I was just trying to nudge it along.'

'An absurd remark.'

'This may provide the motive for Kerr's murder.'

'How?'

'I have been examining the details of the case from all angles . . .'

'I asked for information, not elaboration.'

'Kerr may have visited Son Dragó at a time when there was every probability he would not be observed because Señor Ashton may have been less than the person he appeared to be to most.'

'You have a valid reason for suggesting this?'

'He often sailed to Morocco, but never with his wife, although she went with him on other trips. On his return, he brought back, amongst other things, antique copper caskets. Why the caskets?'

'You do not allow he might appreciate them?'

'Perhaps they were filled with cannabis of a newly developed, considerably more powerful variety. Señor, you may not remember there were several spliffs in Kerr's possession.'

'Do not judge the quality of others' memories by your own.'

'If Kerr bought them locally, he will have known who was dealing in them and learned something which made him think it possible Ashton was importing the cannabis from Morocco. At first sight, this would have seemed ridiculous. Ashton was seemingly wealthy and had no need to take part in so illegal and risky a venture. Was his supposed wealth an invisible cloak? What seems so unlikely, may not be. No one would wonder if the financial chaos of the past years badly hit his income and capital, or that to maintain his luxurious lifestyle he needed to make money quickly.

'Having discovered the truth, Kerr tried to put a black on him, probably for five thousand euros, eight hundred of which had been spent before Ashton decided the blackmailing had to be stopped; the only way, to murder Kerr.'

There was a long silence.

Salas finally said: 'I doubt I have ever before heard the equal of such improbability. What scintilla of proof is there that Señor Ashton suffered any financial distraint before his death? What reason is there for supposing a man of his background and character would, whatever his financial circumstances, even consider indulging in criminal activities? How could he have met Kerr? Is it conceivable he would have wished to have contact with a drug addict?'

'Señor, there were four thousand two hundred euros in cash in Kerr's possession plus the notebook in which was the address of Son Dragó. There is one way of proving I have been talking nonsense.'

'There are several.'

'But wouldn't it be as well to consider that one way, however absurd it might seem to you, and cover one's back?'

'A very regrettable desire.'

'It's so difficult to judge in which way things are likely to go.'

'And for some, in which way they have been. What are the details of the señor's will?'

'I haven't yet—'

'What is the evidence of the cook?'

'I haven't yet—'

'How much longer is the analysis of the contents of the dead man's stomach going to take?'

'The lab said it would be a very lengthy process, and they couldn't give an accurate figure.'

'They said that today?'

'No.'

'Then I suggest you find out when. Logical possibilities need to be examined before illogical ones.' Salas closed the conversation.

The next morning, Alvarez regarded the unopened envelopes on his desk with bored dislike. Official mail was either incoherent, inopportune, or boring. For once, he had misjudged. In one envelope was the authorization for Inspector Alvarez, of the Cuerpo General de Policía, to be given details of the accounts of Señor Ashton, deceased, in Banco Llueso.

He lit a cigarette. Salas must have decided there might be an advantage in having his back covered.

Pagés regarded Alvarez approach with annoyance.

'Good morning, señor,' Alvarez said.

He muttered a return greeting.

'I have come back to ask for details of—'

'You did not understand what I told you?'

'I have an authorization granting me the right to learn certain details regarding the accounts of the late Señor Ashton.'

'Let me see it.'

Alvarez handed him the envelope.

He opened this, brought out a single sheet of paper, read quickly. 'It would have saved time had you bothered to obtain this before previously coming here.'

'I'm afraid I had not realized you would prefer not to save yourself trouble.'

'You should have accepted I would always observe rules and regulations. What exactly do you wish to know?'

'Did Señor Ashton withdraw a large sum in cash in the weeks before his death?'

'A large sum is an indeterminate figure.'

'Something between four thousand and six thousand plus euros.'

Pagés activated the computer on his desk, tapped on the keyboard, studied the screen. 'On the twenty-sixth of last month, he withdrew five thousand euros.'

'In cash?'

'Is that not what you asked?'

'Can you give me the number of the notes?'

'You have very little experience of banking?'

'Quite a lot on the debit side.'

'There is no possibility of our providing the number of a single note.'

Alvarez thanked Pagés for his help, without sounding sarcastic.

NINE

Alvarez phoned Palma. 'Señor, I have spoken to the manager of Llueso Bank. I was right.'

'I might not be so surprised if I knew the subject of your report.'

'I was checking on the money, señor.'

'What money?'

'Payments in cash out of Señor Ashton's bank accounts. You provided the authorization for me.'

'Well?'

'The señor withdrew five thousand euros.'

'Were the notes of high enough denominations for them to be traceable?'

'Unfortunately not.'

'Then it can only be an assumption that this money was paid to Kerr.'

'But if—'

'An assumption which has to be weakened by the fact that there were only four thousand two hundred in his possession when he died.'

'He'll have been spending freely.'

'Eight hundred euros in a short time – on what?'

'Women.'

'You believe it credible in a short time to spend hundreds of euros on a woman?'

'If she's class. Or maybe there were three or four *not* class.'

'The quality of your experience is regrettable. Have you been told it is a grave mistake to bend facts to support a theory?'

'Frequently, señor.'

'Apparently such words have been inadequately understood. There would have been no proof – I emphasize "proof" – that the money came from Señor Ashton had all five thousand been in Kerr's possession. At best, there would have been a reasonable presumption. Due to the difference in totals there can be only the *possibility* the money withdrawn by Señor Ashton was paid to Kerr.'

'He'd bought an expensive locally made sweater and a bottle of expensive malt whisky.'

'You have ascertained their costs?'

'No, señor.'

'Have you spoken to misguided women to learn if he was known to any of them?'

'No, señor.'

'One enquiry I should have expected you to pursue.'

'He arrived on a cheap package holiday and short of cash. If that money did not come from the señor, what was its source?'

'Yet again, you presume a negative indicates a positive. You refuse to consider, for instance, Kerr might have entered a local lottery and won a small prize.'

'Isn't that using an assumption to deny the theory he might have been in the drug trade?'

'The two are totally different in nature, but to explain to you why that is would take too long.'

'Señor. I think we should have the brass caskets from Morocco tested for residue of cannabis. Also, the spliffs which were in Kerr's possession should be sent to the laboratory to find which country the hashish came from.'

'I see no necessity for either course.'

'But—'

'Lateral thinking would remind you that a connection is not always direct. What is the most common motive for all crime? Money. The distribution of Señor Ashton's wealth may well show a strong connection with Kerr's murder.'

'That does seem a little unlikely since—'

'You will accept it is likely and determine the details of the will. Has the cook at Son Dragó provided any information of consequence?'

'As I mentioned, there has not been time—'

'Had you not suffered the possibility Señor Ashton had been engaged in the drug trade, you would have found the time to question her. You will speak to the forensic laboratory and tell them that their delay is hindering our investigation and we need results immediately.'

'I don't suppose that will make any difference.'

'Should I need your opinion, I will ask for it.'

Moments later, Alvarez phoned the laboratory. 'The superior chief is shouting for a result in the Kerr case.'

'That sort of work takes time, full stop.'

'Can you give me an estimate that'll keep him quiet?'

'Tell him he might have an answer by Christmas.'

Not a message that would be passed on.

The front door of Son Dragó was opened by Benavides. 'Good afternoon, inspector. How may I help you?'

'Is Señora Ashton at home?'

'She is.'

'I should like to speak to her if she is willing for me to do so.'

'I will ask. I'm sure you will understand she is very sad and depressed. Please enter, but be kind to wait.'

He went into the hall. The wait was short.

'Perhaps you would like to come this way, inspector?' Benavides said when he reappeared.

Alvarez was shown into a sitting room, less formal than the larger one. There was a large television set, DVD player, cabinet filled with disks, music centre and, at various places, elaborately patterned copper caskets. As Benavides shut the door behind himself, Alvarez brought out of his pocket a handkerchief, opened the nearest casket, and wiped the handkerchief about its interior. Approaching footsteps prevented his intention to repeat the work on a second casket.

Laura, followed by Benavides, entered. 'Señora,' he ponderously announced, 'Inspector Alvarez of the Cuerpo General de Policía.'

'Good afternoon, señora,' Alvarez said. 'May I express my condolences at your tragic loss and my deep regret at having to trouble you.'

'Thank you. Please sit.'

Judging from what Benavides had said, he had expected

her depression to be very marked. Sadness was there, but this was an acceptance, not an emotional rejection, of the tragedy that was life. 'I will be as brief as I can be, señora. I am investigating the death of Colin Kerr. Amongst the items he left was a notebook in which was written the address and telephone number of this house. That gave reason to think he might have come here. Enquiries make this unlikely, but I have to ask if at any time you saw or heard from him?'

'I have had no contact.'

'I'm afraid I have to ask you other questions because we have learned that Kerr did not die from drowning; he may have been poisoned.'

'My God!'

He was unsurprised by her shocked surprise. Even for a policeman, poisoning provided the most premeditated, cruellest death; for a newly widowed woman, he understood it must become a brutal underpinning of her own loss.

Her head was bowed, the fingers of her hands interlaced.

He stood. 'Señora, I apologize very sincerely for the distress I have caused. I will not trouble you any further.'

She did not look up before he left. As he opened the front door, Benavides came into the hall. 'How is the señora?'

'Very upset.'

'You are surprised when you intrude at such a time?'

Alvarez left, walked over to his car. For once, Benavides had spoken like a man, not a servant.

Wednesday morning brought cloud, showers and wind: winter unfolding its wings. Farmers welcomed the rain, tourists complained they were being cheated of their holidays in the sun.

Alvarez had phoned two *abogados* and was about to try a third lawyer when his phone rang.

'Inspector Alvarez,' Ángela Torres said, 'the superior chief wishes to know if you have established the details of Señor Ashton's will?'

'If you put me through, I'll tell him.'

'He is not here which is why I am asking you.'

'Will you say I have had a word with Señora Ashton.'

'She has provided the details of her husband's will?'

'I decided she was in too emotional a state to ask her what they are.'

'The superior chief will be surprised by your decision.'

'Emotion for him being a foreign element?'

'Have you anything to report which he might consider of importance?'

'Not until I discover which *abogado* drew up the will in Spanish.'

'The superior chief is likely to be surprised you have not yet already done so,' she commented before she rang off.

Forty minutes later, he dialled the last number on the list he had written down. The secretary who had a warm voice in contrast to Señorita Torres', referred him to Señor Ramírez.

'We drew up Señor Ashton's will in Spanish as well as English to avoid any of the problems which might occur if there had only been the one. The two are exactly the same.'

'Can you give me the details of the bequests?'

'Not over the phone. If you need to know what they are, you must come here and read the will.'

He sought a way of avoiding the journey to Palma, found none. 'I'll be in tomorrow morning.'

He disliked any large town, but disliked driving in one even more since other drivers were selfish, irresponsible, and potentially dangerous. He had checked the timetable and found he could travel and return by train at reasonable times from Mestara.

At Palma station, he hired a taxi which took him to the offices of Señor Ramírez. One of three secretaries, considerably older than the other two, showed him into a small conference room on two walls of which hung framed certificates of Ramírez's legal qualifications. On the well-polished table were four glossy fashion magazines, an indication that the majority of clients were female. He sat and stared into space.

After ten minutes – no doubt the wait had been to show that Ramírez was a busy man – he was shown into a very well-furnished office. Ramírez shook hands, spoke courteously, but in a manner which signified there would be little room for equality in their brief acquaintance. He was smartly dressed in a suit, his hair was cunningly cut to conceal approaching baldness, his head was egg-shaped, his waist a visible sign of good living. 'Your reason for wishing to read the will?'

'Colin Kerr, an Englishman found in Llueso Bay . . .?'

'Naturally, I have read about that. Do you believe there could have been a connection between the two men?'

'Not directly. But Señor Ashton's wealth might have been responsible for Kerr's murder.'

'Murder!' A civil lawyer, enjoying a happy income from others' domestic unhappiness, Ramírez was disturbed, shocked, by an encounter with crime of such brutality. He fiddled with a paper on the desk. 'You think the will may in some way confirm the possibility?'

'As my superior frequently states, money is the start of almost all crime.'

'It is bitter to learn the harm it can bring.'

Any less bitter than to suffer the harm that lack of it wrought? 'If I may see the will?'

'In English or Castilian?'

'Either.'

Ramírez opened a folder, brought out pages secured by tape, put them down on the far side of the desk. Alvarez reached forward, picked them up, and read, wondered why no legal document was ever written in plain, everyday language. He looked up. 'Have you a sheet of paper and a pen or pencil?'

'You have brought neither with you?'

A weak attempt to underline his inefficiency. He was handed a sheet of A4 and a ballpoint pen, and he rested the paper on the elaborately inlaid desk and copied out pertinent details from the will.

'Do you have a preliminary valuation of the señor's estate?' he asked as he returned the will.

'Not yet.'

'But you'll have an estimate?'

There was a pause before Ramírez answered. 'The figure I'll give is of no legal value. The total will be roughly seven million euros.'

Alvarez's thoughts wandered. Recently, politicians spending

other people's money had spoken of billions as once they would have mentioned millions. To an inspector, one million, let alone seven, still signified wealth beyond his comprehension.

Back in his office, Alvarez reread the bequests in the will. They were straightforward and generous. Benavides and Beatriz were each to receive ten thousand euros in return for their loyal service; García, ten thousand; Inés, Patera and Valles (took time to remember that Patera and Valles were the dailies and he still had not questioned them), one thousand each; Port Llueso, five thousand to be used at the council's discretion; two named charities, five thousand each; Son Dragó and any capital or income not specified, to his beloved wife.

As, phone to his ear, he waited to speak to Salas, he watched a gecko climb up to the window, then 'freeze' as it looked over the edge of the window sill. How long before it decided it would be safe to move? Ten euros it would be at least one minute.

'Yes?' Salas said.

The gecko went over the window sill. Forty-eight seconds. He had never been a successful gambler, even when betting against himself. 'I have spoken to Señora Ashton.'

'What have you learned?'

'She never met Kerr or spoke to him over the telephone. She does not believe her husband knew him.'

'She told you the terms of her husband's will?'

'No.'

'Why not?'

'I did not ask her what they are.'

'You considered it unnecessary to pursue so obvious a course?'

'She was too emotionally upset.'

'Her emotions are of no significance in such a case.'

'Had you seen her, señor, you would not say that. At least, I hope you would not.'

'You insinuate I lack sympathy?'

'Perhaps that depends to whom you are speaking.'

'You will return to speak to her and demand to see the will.'

'That won't be necessary.'

'You are under the misapprehension that you are in command of the investigation?'

'I spoke to Señor Ramírez.'

'Would it trouble you to identify him?'

'After many enquiries, I learned it was his firm which had drawn up Señor Ashton's will.'

'Unnecessary enquiries, had you overcome your reluctance to ask Señora Ashton for the information. What are the details?'

Alvarez read out the names and amounts of the legacies.

'Have you not forgotten one name?'

'I think not, señor.'

'Did you not identify the nephew, Browyer, as a suspect because he would inherit under the will?'

'Yes, but he is not named and there is evidence he knew he would be disinherited.'

'Then you can no longer consider him a suspect.'

'I think he must remain one.'

'Why?'

'It is possible he killed the señor because he was *not* in the will.'

'Then we must consider all the other persons who are not included. A task at which even Hercules would have baulked.'

'I don't think you understand.'

'You are correct.'

'It's probable that compared to his uncle's style of living, Browyer's life was very reduced and dull. Since the señor had told him over the phone he would give him no more money, this must have inflamed Browyer's sense of injustice. He may have been sufficiently resentful to murder the señor.'

'Your imagination seems to have no limit.'

'There's the other possibility that having heard about the drug running from Morocco, he was blackmailing the señor.'

'That is a possibility which lacks even a shred of what you might mistakenly choose to term evidence.'

'When I went to Son Dragó, to speak to the señora, I was shown into a sitting room in which were several of the copper caskets the señor brought back from Morocco. I used a hand-kerchief to wipe around the inside of one of these and will send that, and the spliffs, to the laboratory to ask them to determine where the marijuana came from and if there was any trace of it on the handkerchief.'

'As a Mallorquin, you clearly lack the slightest knowledge of how a visitor does, or does not, behave.'

TEN

Benavides held open the front door for Alvarez to enter Son Dragó. 'I wish to apologize for my unwarranted remarks, inspector.'

'They're forgotten. How is the señora?'

'Very troubled. She refused breakfast and ate hardly any lunch. Beatriz was so worried, she called the doctor. He said the señora should have a sedative; she is now sleeping.'

After Juana-María died, Alvarez had suffered times when he had not wanted to eat or drink, but instead, perversely, to live with the memories which intensified his mental pain. 'There is no need to disturb her since I came to have a word with Beatriz.'

'She is in the kitchen, preparing a meal in the hope it will tempt the señora to eat when she is awake. I will ask Beatriz to speak to you in the staff sitting-room.'

'And interrupt her cooking? I'll have a word in the kitchen.'

'Then it is to be hoped everything has gone as intended.' Benavides smiled – the first time Alvarez had seen any expression but one of a solemn sense of duty. 'When things go wrong, she is unbearable.'

'The sign of a good cook.'

The kitchen had large work surfaces, a refrigerator which delivered ice cubes, a deep-freeze, food processors of different shapes and sizes, a bread maker, two more machines which he failed to identify with a quick glance, and a double-oven cooker with gas-fed rings on the top. The scent of cooking was strong and sweet.

'Something is going to have a five-star taste,' he said.

Beatriz looked briefly at him. '*Me a la Mallorquina*. You want something?'

To enjoy some *Me*. It was quite a time since Dolores had cooked the dish – one which must please the most pernickety epicurean. 'I'm Inspector Alvarez.'

'Who else would invade my kitchen when I am cooking?'
She was built on a generous scale and lacked attractive features;
nevertheless, she reminded him of Dolores when cooking
because of her disdainful superiority, dislike of any interruption, focused attention on what she was doing.

'It seemed better to have a word with you here rather than
disturb your work. My cousin says that a minute's inattention
can ruin hours of work.'

'She is right.'

He watched her fry garlic in hot lard. 'I'll try not to interrupt you at a vital moment.'

'You are not already doing so?'

'Hopefully, not to any great extent.'

'Move.'

He moved away from the central table on which lamb, cut
into cubes, was on a chopping board. She picked that up,
carefully dropped the lamb into the garlic, adjusted the height
of the gas flame, stirred with a wooden spoon.

'As Manuel must have told you—'

'The salt.'

An open jar of sea salt was on the table. He passed it to
her, and she extracted a pinch, scattered this over the meat.

'I've been trying to find out if Kerr, the man who died in
the bay, ever came here. That seems possible because he had
noted the address in a notebook and—'

'Onions.'

Chopped onions were on a plate, which he gave her. She
added these to the contents of the frying pan, then a couple
of spoonfuls of flour, covered the mixture with red wine and
water.

'When Manuel can't respond to the front door bell for some
reason, I gather Inés does.'

'If I cannot.'

'She is reluctant to do so?'

'She is very nervous and uneasy in the presence of strangers.
She suffers an unfortunate experience.'

'What is that?'

'Nothing to do with you.' She stirred the contents of the
frying pan, added a little more flour, some leaves of mint.

'It seems Señor Ashton was a good employer.'

'Yes.'

'Easy-going?'

'When someone knew his job.'

'Generous?'

'If needed, very generous.'

'You're thinking of García's daughter?'

'That and of many other occasions.'

'Did he smoke?'

'No.' She turned down the gas, covered the frying pan.

'Were you ever aware of a lingering smell in the house which was not like ordinary cigarette smoke?'

'No. Are you finished? I have to prepare *Amargos* for the señora. They were her favourite sweet before the señor died, and I hope they will help to refresh her appetite. You have any more questions?'

'I don't think so.'

'Then you can clear out of my kitchen.'

He left. It was an article in every cook's faith that it was 'her kitchen'. In a palace, no doubt the chef worked in 'his' kitchen.

He drove back to Llueso and Carrer Joan Rives, had to park well away from home. The air was cooling quickly, yet he found the walk enervating.

Jaime sat at the table in the sitting/dining room, glass, a bottle of Soberano and an ice bucket in front of himself. He indicated the glass in front of Alvarez's seat, pushed the bottle across the table. Alvarez sat, poured himself a drink, added ice.

'You're late,' Jaime said.

'I've had to work flat out.'

There was a call from the kitchen. 'A position in which your work no doubt is frequently performed.'

Jaime spoke in a low voice. 'When I got back, I told her I was overwhelmed with all the work, and all she could say was that if I did what she has to do here in running the house, I wouldn't last half the morning.'

'Female self-deception.'

'And what are you now deceiving yourself about?' Dolores asked as she came through the bead curtain.

Alvarez had spoken a fraction too loudly; she would hear a dewdrop fall on cotton wool. 'That I reckon my work is of consequence because it is concerned with maintaining law and order.'

'Which is why Susana's car was broken into and the radio stolen along with all the shopping.' She returned into the kitchen.

Alvarez poured himself another drink.

The telephone rang first thing on Thursday. 'Juan here, forensic laboratory. Re Colin Kerr, deceased. We have identified the poison. Hydrocyanic acid.'

'Prussic acid?'

'In a nutshell.'

'I've read it's very powerful stuff.'

'Start a drink and you likely won't finish it. You will collapse, frantically gasp for breath as you seem to be in the grip of convulsions. Seconds for you will be as hours to another, each hour gripped in an agony for which no torturer could provide its equal.'

'Where's it likely to have come from?'

'Maybe industry. It's used in fumigation, photography, engraving, gold and silver processing. Not to forget bitter almonds; their oil contains up to ten per cent.'

'As much as that?'

'Eat too many and it's goodbye. Of course, they're not nearly so deadly as the raw acid, and there'll be time to tell relatives how much you dislike them. Are you interested in the symptoms?'

'No.'

'The throat contracts, mouth burns, retching and vomiting begin, violent pains grip the heart . . .'

He ceased to listen until the list of possible symptoms concluded. So much better never to know what could happen to one's defenceless body.

'In this case, normally the provisional diagnosis would have been quickly given due to smell and appearance, but the relatively long immersion in water prevented that. Anything more you'd like to know?'

'Not about prussic acid.'

'Worried because there's a bitter almond tree nearby? I don't suppose you realize how much poison grows all around the place. For instance—'

'I'd rather not know.'

'Lily of the valley, meadow saffron, hemlock, oleander, datura and many more. Then there are the mushrooms – amanita phalloides, the Death Cap – which can be as deadly as a snake's venom.'

He liked mushrooms. *Truita d'esclata-sangs* was an omelette for which a gourmet might offer his soul. But since one seldom knew who had picked the mushrooms, how could one be certain that he – or, more likely, a she – had not made a mistake?

'If that's all you want, I'll get back to checking some potatoes.'

'Why are you looking at them?'

'To find out if solanine poisoning was responsible for the grave illness of a five year old.'

'Potatoes can't be dangerous; they're eaten by everyone all the time.'

'The plant belongs to the family which includes Deadly Nightshades. The child saw some potatoes which were sprouting, thought the green shoots looked appetizing and unfortunately ate some.'

'But . . . ordinary potatoes surely must be all right?'

'So long as there aren't any green areas which are eaten. If you have two or three spuds and suddenly become anxious, dizzy, suffer facial pallor, twitching of the limbs and hallucinate, you've eaten some green potato. But don't panic. It's unlikely to be fatal.' The assistant laughed before he cut the connection.

Dolores must surely cut off any green area of a potato, but would the cook in a restaurant where profit was more important than the life of a customer? One could pay eight euros for a *menu del dia* and not live to finish the third course . . . The laboratory assistant had not mentioned grapes. Because they had to be safe, or had he forgotten them? If they were sprayed too heavily against botrytis, could the wine and brandy become charged with a poison . . .?

The phone rang.

'Inspector Alvarez? Hotel Clients' ID shows that Charles Browyer is staying at Hotel Floris in Playa Nueva.'

He forgot to thank the other because his mind could not lose the picture of a garden inhabited by skeletons.

Playa Nueva's reputation was due to clever publicists. The longest sandy beach, cleaned every day; hotels of luxury quality or for those on budgets; restaurants serving dishes for all tastes . . .

Alvarez viewed it as a small fishing village which had been ground underfoot by developers.

He drove past a seemingly endless parade of tourist shops, cafés, restaurants, supermarkets, estate agents. Hotel Floris was on the inland side of the coast road and lay behind and in the shadow of a much larger hotel. Tourists would have read in the brochures that the sea was within five minutes' walk; it was not mentioned that the main coast road had to be crossed, and with the constant, heavy flow of traffic, five could become ten, fifteen, or even more.

The reception clerk's manner belied the promise of the hotel welcoming tourists. 'You want what?'

'To know if Señor Browyer is in his room.'

One of the four phones rang; the desk clerk answered the call, talked flirtatiously in Americanized English. Alvarez waited patiently until the clerk began to list the pleasures of lying on the beach in moonlight; he reached over and pressed down the stop bar.

'What d'you think you're doing?' the desk clerk demanded in Mallorquin, adding a couple of expressive adjectives.

'Saving a young lady's virtue.'

'It's none of your business.'

'Cuerpo.'

The desk clerk attempted to show the contempt for authority which had become a mark of democracy. 'That doesn't give you the right to muck up my call.'

'It allows me not to have my work held up by some panting youth from Laraix.'

Annoyance became uneasiness. 'How d'you know where I'm from?'

To a Lluesean, the Laraix accent was easily recognized, and, for a reason few remembered, the inhabitants of the two villages viewed each other with dislike and contempt. Alvarez did not answer the question.

'What . . . What d'you want?'

'As I said, to know if Señor Browyer is in his room.'

'He'll more likely be eating.'

'A late breakfast?'

'Lunch.'

'This early?'

'Some of 'em would like it even earlier, being so hungry-gutted.'

'Get on to his room.'

The clerk checked numbers, dialled. There was no answer.

'See if he is in the dining room.' He might have to wait for Browyer to finish his meal. 'What's on the menu?'

'Fish soup, then cold meats or beef stew, salad, chips, and a sweet.'

A half-formed suggestion was abandoned. He would not eat there however long he had to wait. Fish soup could come out of a tin, cold meats be yesterday's leftovers, beef tough and tasteless even in a stew, olive oil from a fourth pressing, chips from green potatoes. 'I'll wait to talk to him. Will you organize a coñac with ice only?'

The clerk hesitated, then spoke over an internal telephone.

Six minutes later, a waiter entered the foyer, a frosting glass in his hand. He looked at the desk clerk, correctly interpreted the nod, crossed to Alvarez and handed him the glass.

'How much?' Alvarez asked.

'I understood it was on the house.'

Almost certainly a misunderstanding. The brandy was of very medium quality, but drinkable. He was considering whether hotel hospitality would support a second one when people began to leave the dining room. He walked over to the reception desk. 'Do you know Señor Browyer?'

'Can't say I do.'

'Call out his name.'

Browyer was the last to leave. He came through the doorway,

laughing at something he had said to the man beside him who looked bored, not amused. When he heard his name, he stopped, uncertain and uneasy. He walked slowly to the reception desk. 'What's the problem?' With blustering bonhomie, he said: 'Have I won the lottery or has Miss World phoned?'

'Inspector Alvarez wants to talk to you,' the desk clerk answered.

'An inspector in what?'

'The Cuerpo.'

'What's that?'

'The detective division of the police force.'

'What . . .? They've already found out I robbed the bank?' He laughed, sounding like the neighing of a horse.

'I don't think any bank has recently been robbed,' Alvarez said.

'Just a funny. I mean, I wouldn't know how to begin.'

'As you have been told, I wish to have a word with you.'

'But about what?'

'That will become clear.'

'Then I suppose we'd better go into what they call the lounge.'

'In order to have privacy, it will be best to go up to your room.'

'You're . . .' He stopped.

A lift, initially hesitant and then vibrating, took them to the fourth floor. Room 414, a single, faced the much larger hotel and would enjoy sunshine for only a small part of the day. The bed had not yet been made, and a pair of pyjamas with a tricoloured pattern trailed across the pillows. A half-empty bottle of Gordon's and a dirty glass were on the small chest-of-drawers. On the bedside table was a paperback, the multicoloured cover of which featured two men sunbathing on a sandy beach.

'Is there some kind of trouble?' Browyer weakly asked.

Alvarez sat on the edge of the bed. 'I'm investigating the death of Colin Kerr.'

'Isn't . . . isn't that the name of the man who drowned?'

'Yes.'

The door opened, and a maid entered, came to a sudden

stop. She looked at them, left, shut the door behind herself. Alvarez briefly considered hurrying out and explaining the true situation to her.

'You can't think . . . I never met the man.' Browyer's blustering had given way to uneasiness. 'I swear it was nothing to do with me. It can't be, I didn't know him.'

'You are a nephew of the late Señor Ashton?'

'Yes, but—'

'Are you here because you had hoped to borrow more money from him?'

'Why do you think that?'

'Cows don't shed their horns. Do you expect to benefit under your uncle's will?'

'He disinherited me. Just because . . . He was living like it was seventy years ago.'

'What exactly do you mean by that?'

'He thought . . . thought it was a sin. I tried to explain. But she wouldn't let him understand. She hates me.'

'You are referring to Señora Ashton?'

'Of course I am.'

'You believe she dislikes you because of your sexuality?'

'Because I know how it went.'

'What went?'

He poured himself a drink of neat gin. 'She made eyes at him in the hospital so he had her as a day nurse at home. There, she hotted him up until he married her. If the old fool had had any sense, he'd have got what he wanted for a few quid.'

'I have met the señora. For her, initially the relationship rested solely on sympathy.'

'Believe that and you know sod-all about women. He'd lost his wife, but Laura stroked his brow and had him wriggling like a fifteen year old.'

'Those who knew them before the señor died have repeatedly said they had a great affection for each other.'

'I'm his nephew, but he leaves me nothing, and she gets everything.'

'The will is not yet public. How do you know you have been disinherited?'

'What's that matter?'

'You have a reason for not answering?'

'A bloke told me.'

'Who was he?'

'A clerk in a lawyer's office.'

'Señor Ramírez's office in Palma?

'I can't remember.'

'Where did you meet the clerk?'

After a long pause, Browyer answered: 'At the office.'

'Whose name you have forgotten. Why did he tell you?'

'We . . . saw each other a couple of times and . . .' He drank eagerly.

'Did you often ask your uncle for money?'

'I'd got nothing, and he was bloody rich. The house here, properties in other countries, luxury car, yacht, and God knows what else.'

'You resented his wealth?'

'It wouldn't have hurt him to pass something on.'

'When you came to the island, did you stay at Son Dragó?'

'Until he suggested it would be more convenient for everyone if I stayed in a hotel. The staff were always complaining about me. They couldn't understand they were just servants.'

'That didn't stop you coming to the island since you hoped your frequent requests for money would eventually bear fruit.'

'It wasn't like that.'

'How was it, then?'

There was no answer.

'Were you ever aware that the señor smoked reefers?'

'Did what? He'd as soon have been caught in a massage parlour as smoking dope.'

'You'll know what smoked cannabis smells like.'

'If you're saying . . . If someone had smoked it, it would have been her.'

'No doubt there are another dozen faults of which you'd like to accuse her, but I've not the time or wish to listen.'

He left. It had been time wasted in the company of an insecure, jealous, frustrated man.

Jaime's greeting as he entered the dining room was: 'You're so late, the kids have eaten everything.'

'You had twice what I did,' Juan, a half-peeled apple in his hand, protested.

'That's why he's got so big a tummy,' Isabel observed.

'How many times do I need to tell you two that it is rude to make personal remarks?' Dolores asked sharply.

'You told Daddy he'd get even fatter if he had any more.'

'That was a reminder, not a personal comment. Enrique, your meal is in the oven. It will be all right, but not as good as had you returned on time.'

'I had to talk to people in Playa Nueva.'

'That prevented you phoning to tell me you would be late home?'

He went into the kitchen, brought out of the oven a well-filled plateful of *Estofat de bou*. He briefly, superficially, felt sorry for the tourists at Hotel Floris who had been condemned to a meal of cold tinned soup, leathery beef stew, and a taste-less sponge covered with a cream mixture from a spray can. He returned to the dining room.

Juan stared at Alvarez's plate. 'If you eat all that, you'll burst.'

'What have I just told you?' Dolores snapped.

'That wasn't a personal comment, it was a kind of reminder,' Juan answered.

Jaime laughed. 'Well said!'

'Isabel and Juan, outside and play until it's time for school,' she ordered.

They hurried into the *entrada*; slammed the front door shut.

Dolores faced Jaime. Her words were coated in ice. 'As a parent, you should wish your son to behave well, not encourage him to act like a tramp.'

'But it was sharp of him,' Jaime muttered.

'My mother was correct.'

'Was she ever anything else?'

'You might manage to talk sense if you would only drink very little, but that possibility is too improbable for us ever to know.'

'That's a nice thing for a wife to say!'

'It was your mother-in-law who said it.'

'It's a wonder you ever married me.'

'*She* would have called it a mystery. Have you finished? If so, pass me your plate, knife, fork and glass.'

He passed the first three.

'Your glass.'

'I am going to have a little more wine.'

'You *were*.' She collected up glasses, plates and cutlery, carried them into the kitchen.

Jaime said: 'Enrique, did your parents ever discuss her? I mean, what kind of a person she was?' He indicated the kitchen.

'My mother used to say she was very kind-hearted, ready to help anyone, but could be a bit sharp occasionally. You were asking for trouble when you laughed at Juan's remark.'

'How was I to know it would annoy her?'

There were some for whom experience was no tutor.

ELEVEN

He had enjoyed a restful siesta, and it was well after five when Alvarez drove up to Son Dragó. García was using a fork to spread dung around a white and red multi-flowered hibiscus. He dug the tines into the soil, softened by watering, rested his hands on the handle and watched Alvarez approach.

'Mule?' Alvarez asked as he pointed to the contents of the wheelbarrow.

'Horse.'

'Best of the lot. Where d'you get it?'

'Riding stables.'

'Which ones?'

García shrugged his shoulders. One did not provide information from which an advantage could be gained by another.

Alvarez regarded the hibiscus. 'I don't think I've seen so many flowers on a single bush before.'

García used an upturned mattock to transfer horse dung.

'D'you remember talking about the almond trees at the bottom of the garden?'

'No.'

'What kind are they?'

'Prunus dulcis mostly.'

'Doesn't say anything to me.'

'Does much?'

'White blossom or pink?'

'Both.'

'So some are bitter almonds?'

'If you say.'

'You don't know?'

'I don't try to tell when someone thinks he knows what he's talking about.'

'The wind's getting sharpish, so what about moving to the garden shed?'

They walked to the small building, its wooden exterior marked by sun, wind, and rain. Once seated, Alvarez offered a pack of Marlboro cigarettes.

'Know someone who runs 'em in?' García asked as he took one.

'You think I'd knowingly buy smuggled cigarettes?'

'If you got the chance.'

'How many of the trees are growing bitter almonds?'

'Four.'

'A dangerous mistake, surely?'

'Why?'

'Doesn't the Señor hold open days when people can wander around the grounds after paying a couple of euros which go to charity? Some stupid oaf might try to eat a bitter almond, not knowing what it is.'

'I knock 'em all down and clear up before the open day in September. Anyway, there's always a notice saying not to eat any fallen nuts.'

'I haven't seen a notice.'

'Because it ain't there. Move it after I've cleared the trees and burned all the almonds.'

'Why not get rid of the trees?'

'The señor liked the different coloured blossom.'

Alvarez was about to remark that it seemed a dubious pleasure when he remembered the laboratory assistant's long list of dangerous plants. Looking through the open doorway, he could see several oleander bushes. 'When did you knock them down this year?'

'Several weeks ago.'

'It's difficult to strip a tree, so maybe some were left?'

'Not when I've finished.' García stood, reached over to a small cane basket, brought out a bottle of 504 and a glass. 'I'd likely offer you some, but you won't want the common stuff.'

'You imagine I drink only French cognac?'

'Why not, when you know someone who runs cigarettes and you'll get it cheap?'

Alvarez was handed a well-filled glass. He raised it in greeting, drank. 'I've asked if you ever saw Kerr in the garden.'

'More times than a hen cackles after laying.'

'If you were sitting in here, you wouldn't see someone at the far end, by the almond trees.'

'I only waste time when an inspector moans about the cold.'

'You always have your *merienda* outside even when it's raining and twice as cold as now?'

There was no answer.

'So there's time, every day, when a man could help himself to bitter almonds still on the tree or fallen to the ground and missed by you, when you wouldn't see him?'

'Look through that.' García pointed at the window, beyond which both the approach to the house and the track to the end of the promontory were visible. 'No one's been along since a German couple dug up the land with those bloody stupid walking poles.'

'How did you react?'

'Think I invited them in here?'

Alvarez finished his drink and as he waited to be offered a second one, dismissed García's claim that he spent little time in the hut. To sit and look out at a rare Mallorquin garden which stretched almost the length of the promontory, the bay, and the sea beyond the headlands, would be an irresistible temptation. 'Did the señor often talk to you about the garden?'

'Every day when he was fit enough to walk around.'

'Would he sometimes be smoking?'

'No.'

'Did you ever think he might be on marijuana?'

'A man like him into dope? You're as daft as Old Albert, who only found out he couldn't walk on water when he drowned.'

'It's difficult to tell what a man will do, and I have to consider all possibilities.'

'Then you'll consider them on your own on account of me wanting to do the work I'm paid for.' He brought the bottle of brandy out of the basket.

About time, was Alvarez's silent comment.

García held the bottle steady with one hand, used a pencil to mark on the label the level of the brandy, replaced the bottle. He left before Alvarez could find the words to express his opinion of such miserly suspicion.

If the coming telephone conversation became extended, he would not return home in time to relax and enjoy a brandy before the meal. But if he didn't ring . . .

'Who is calling?' Ángela Torres said, in the tones of an official demanding a passport at a border control point.

'Inspector Alvarez, señorita. Is the superior chief in his office?'

'Why do you always ask?'

'He might have been called away on some matter.'

'Superior Chief Salas is only summoned on matters important enough to warrant someone of his rank and standing.'

Spinsters of a certain age were often said to regard their bosses with stars in their eyes; in her case, she probably included a halo. 'I should like to speak to him.'

There was a wait, then a sharp: 'Yes?'

'Señor, in connection with the case of Colin Kerr, deceased, found dead in Llueso Bay on the first of the month . . .'

'What was the direction of the wind?'

'I don't know. But does that matter?'

'It does not.'

'Then . . . why do you ask, señor?'

'If I pose a question which is obviously irrelevant, it is a criticism of the unnecessary detail I am being offered.'

'But you so often . . . It would be easier for me if I could distinguish which of your questions was meaningless.'

'And I should find it easier if I could decide whether it is ignorance or insolence which dictates your speech. Why are you phoning?'

'I have revisited Son Dragó and spoken to García. I asked him—'

'Who is García?'

Certain words danced on his tongue, but he managed to quieten them. 'The gardener. Four of the almond trees produce bitter almonds. I said I was surprised they didn't cut them down for the sake of safety, but it seems the señor used to like to see the contrasting colours of blossom.'

'A dendrologist might find the information of interest; I do not.'

'The bitter almond is a source of prussic acid.'

'A scientific discovery of which you have become aware?'

'It is important.'

'To someone ignorant enough to eat them.'

'But Kerr was poisoned by prussic acid.'

'Your authority for saying that?'

'It's what the laboratory reported.'

'I am interested finally to be told this.'

'I mentioned it when I said I had questioned Señor Browyer.'

'You are consistent in that you have reported neither fact.'

He thought back. The intention had definitely been there, but his time in the garden shed at Son Dragó had been very relaxing.

'No doubt, you considered the information of insufficient importance to mention until now?'

'There is so much going on, señor.'

'Is any of it concerned with your work?'

'Señor Browyer denied knowing Kerr. I've no reason to think he's lying.'

'Why?'

'It needs mental strength knowingly to poison someone; Browyer clearly has very little. To accept that when the victim swallows the poison, he is on the brink of hell and within seconds will fall and suffer unendurable agonies for an immeasurable time . . .'

'If he endures them, they are not unendurable. Resist the urge to empty a dictionary of histrionic words.'

'I asked him if he had ever knowingly seen Señor Ashton smoking a spliff. He denied the possibility. And it is almost a rule that drug dealers seldom sample their own products or they become victims.'

'You still are unable to accept that Señor Ashton, with his wealth and position, was the most unlikely of men to enter the drug trade?'

'How else can one explain the facts? Kerr received five thousand euros from Señor Ashton and the—'

'I have previously pointed out that that is an assumption, not proven fact. As is the proposition to pass a handkerchief around a second casket since this might expose that the señor had a part in the drug trade.'

'But . . .'

'The laboratory failed to trace the slightest indication of marijuana, or any other drug, on the handkerchief you sent them.'

'How do you know that?'

'Their report is reasonably intelligible.'

'I didn't know they'd given it.'

'I informed you of the fact.'

'No, señor, you did not. Had I known about the report, I would not have suggested a second casket, nor would I have questioned staff about the señor's smoking. Just as the pressure of work caused me to delay my report, it must have done the same to you. Part of the trouble is that *I* asked the lab to test the handkerchief, but they reported the result to *you*. Had they got back on to me when saying what was the nature of the poison—'

'You blame them for your mistakes?'

'I don't think anyone can be blamed for honestly forgetting.'

'But for dishonestly forgetting? The laboratory found that the marijuana in the cigarettes from the dead man's possession did not come from Morocco.'

'Then it was probably from Algeria and transported there.'

'It was grown in England.'

'Impossible!'

'A rash comment, even if made by a man such as myself. With ever-increasing frequency, it is grown indoors under a bank of electric light bulbs. You should now be able to understand your theory that Señor Ashton had any part in the drug trade is ridiculous, as is your suggestion to pursue the matter.'

'I did not know about the nature of the tobacco in the cigarettes.'

'You were informed by me some time ago.'

'I'm sure you didn't tell me, señor.'

'I shall ask my friend, the eminent psychologist, what a continual denial of fact signifies.'

The call over, Alvarez opened the bottom drawer in the desk. It seemed to be in keeping that there was only one small drink remaining in the bottle of Soberano.

TWELVE

The next morning, seated in his office, Alvarez wondered if, as Salas held, the motive for Kerr's murder was money. It no longer made sense to consider Ashton had had any part in the drug trade. Then Kerr could not have learned this and blackmailed him over the fact. Yet if the money Ashton had drawn from the bank had not followed blackmail, for what possible reason would he have given it to Kerr?

Was it coincidence that the money in Kerr's possession had been within eight hundred euros of the five thousand Ashton had drawn? To explain, as he had, the difference between the two sums by saying the money had been spent on wine, women, a pullover and a bottle of malt whisky, was not only difficult to substantiate – not that he had yet tried to do so – but unlikely. There were still many female tourists who would welcome the company of an attractive man and not name the cost.

Because of his belief in the possibility of drug smuggling, he had tended to overlook the bequests the staff were to receive. Ten thousand might not seem enough to encourage a murder, but these were constantly being committed for stupidly small amounts. Could one believe stately Benavides would murder for such a sum, or for ten times as much? But who could know the desires, fears, hopes, and guidelines of another human? The council of Port Llueso had been willed five thousand euros. Pleasant, but absurd, to imagine the council members agreeing to murder Ashton in order to gain that amount, that each member would trust his or her colleagues to divide the money equally.

Let the money be the motive. Logically, Laura Ashton had to be the prime suspect. She had become rich. He had learned she was a woman of much compassion, but no man should believe he could correctly judge a woman's character when she could deceive with a smile, speak love with a dagger in her hand. A woman would believe a younger man who swore she was more beautiful than the stars seen from the crest of Puig Major. But how could she have had any cause to wish Kerr dead? The staff unanimously agreed he had never visited the house; she had nursed her husband with the strength of love. Was there an as yet unknown man of her own age who, unknown to everyone else, had ingratiated himself into her affections? Had the staff, loyal to her, lied about there being any such companion? He was a damned fool to ask himself the questions. Was he not convinced she was as true and loyal as any woman could be? Yet he had accepted a man could not hope correctly to assess a woman's true character . . .

He looked at his watch. *Merienda* time.

'You're looking less than lively,' was Roca's greeting as he reached the bar in Club Llueso.

'I've been turning circles in my mind,' he answered.

'Small ones?'

'A coñac, a café cortado and respect for your customers.'

'How do I go about finding that?'

Coffee and brandy were put down in front of him. He drank. Women were, by nature, devious, but Laura Ashton was an exception and he was ashamed to have doubted her, to have thought she could betray her husband when he was alive and perhaps his memory after his death.

'Why so deep in thought? Thinking of meeting a lady who mistakes you for a gentleman?' Roca asked.

'Another coñac and café.'

'Some people say "please" when they want something.'

'Not when they know the service they'll get here.'

'When you meet your dream woman she'll continue looking for her dream man.'

'Yes?' Ángela Torres demanded.

'I'd like a word with the superior chief,' Alvarez answered.

'You are who?'

He told her.

'Yes?' Salas' curt question was clearly the origin of his secretary's manner.

'Inspector Alvarez, señor. Having considered the facts in the Kerr case, I think it could be informative to ask the police in England if he was known to them.'

'On what grounds?'

'The pathologist was of the opinion the scar on Kerr's neck might well have been caused by a broken bottle.'

'And if that was so?'

'The use of a broken bottle in a fight surely means rough company. That would indicate a different background from what we have so far considered. It might well be that the money in Kerr's possession came from criminal activity in England in which others were involved. He stole all the money and fled. He was traced to here and killed in revenge.'

'Another theory based on the most unlikely proposition.'

'I don't see why you should say that.'

'You have forgotten the evidence strongly suggests the money was provided by Señor Ashton?'

'You have said one should not assume that.'

'If they had killed Kerr out of revenge, they would first have searched for the stolen money and found it amongst his possessions in the villa.'

'I still think it would be worth contacting the English police to learn if Kerr had a criminal background.'

'It is surprising you have not found a way of introducing elephants into the case. Have you learned anything of consequence from Patera or Valles?'

Alvarez stared at the jumble of papers on the desk as he struggled to put persons to the names. Eureka! The two local women with part-time jobs at Son Dragó. 'I fear, señor, I had not yet managed to find the time to question them. I was on my way to do so when you phoned me.'

'You phoned *me*. In future, try to offer an excuse for not doing your job which is not quite so familiar.'

'María and Raquel's addresses?' Benavides said as he stood in the hall of Son Dragó. 'I wouldn't know, but Beatriz will.'

'And if you'd also ask her if she has a telephone number for each of them.'

'Very well. If you will—' He stopped as Laura came into the hall. 'Inspector Alvarez, señora, has arrived.'

She faced Alvarez. 'Good morning, inspector.'

He returned the greeting. She appeared to be more at ease with grief than when he had previously seen her; had taken more trouble over her appearance.

Benavides said: 'In the course of his investigation, señora, the inspector is seeking details of Patera's and Valles's residences. Perhaps the inspector may stay here until I have had a word with Beatriz?' He spoke as if referring to a scruffy plumber who had come to mend a burst pipe.

She had not missed the nature of his tone. 'It'll be more comfortable in the sitting room. And since it is the right time of the day, inspector, perhaps you would like to join me in having a drink?'

'Thank you, señora, I would.'

'What you would like?'

He gained perverse pleasure in knowing Benavides would resent waiting on him, despite his obsequious politeness. 'May I have a coñac with ice, please?'

'And I'll have some champagne, Manuel.' She spoke to Alvarez: 'If you would like to come through?'

They entered the large, luxuriously furnished room, through the picture windows of which was a three-quarters' circular view of mountains, bay, headlands, open sea, and the port.

'Do sit, inspector.'

She was one of the very few Englishwomen from a wealthy background who had spoken to him on terms of equality.

'You think María or Raquel may be able to help you?'

'I rather doubt that, señora, but I need to question anyone who might, however unlikely it is.'

'You have not yet been able to learn much about the unfortunate man?'

'I'm afraid not.'

'Even though I do not know who he was, I was shocked to learn what had happened.'

Benavides entered with a tray on which was a flute, a bottle of champagne in an ice bucket, and a glass containing brandy and ice. He placed flute and ice bucket on the embroidered runner on the occasional table at the side of her chair, skilfully opened the bottle of Veuve Cliquot without losing a drop, quarter filled the flute, allowed the bubbles to dissipate, filled the glass, replaced the bottle in the ice bucket. He handed the glass of brandy to Alvarez with notable lack of grace. 'Is that all, señora?'

'Thank you. Have you been able to learn what the inspector wishes to know?'

'Beatriz is writing down both addresses and phone numbers. Shall I bring them through when she has finished?'

'Yes, please.'

He left.

'*Salud*!' She raised her glass.

'A hundred years, señora.'

'I always think it would be disturbing to live that long. One would meet so much sorrow.'

'I am afraid that is true.' As he had learned from many fewer years.

She sipped the champagne, replaced the flute on the table. 'Is there a family?'

'I beg your pardon?'

'Has the dead man left a family who will have to come to terms with the tragedy?'

'We know so little about him, I can't answer.'

'Then one has to hope he did not.' She paused. 'Have you been in the police during all your working life?'

'My father farmed some land he had inherited, and when old enough, I helped him. But it was not large enough to provide for me as well as my parents, so I had to find a job.'

'Would you have preferred to carry on farming?'

'Were I to win the lottery, that is what I would do.'

'Rather than lead a life of luxury?'

'It would give me pleasure to sow and to reap, to plant saplings which grow into fruitful trees, to have a large flock of sheep . . . I am sorry, señora, I am boring you.'

'No, inspector, you are not. I understand what you mean by the pleasure of producing. In the winter I sometimes see in one of the garden centres a bare shrub with only a photo of what it will look like when flowering. I sometimes buy and try to plant it myself, but Felipe always finds an excuse for doing the planting himself.'

'As we say, the sweetest orange is grown by the speaker.'

Benavides entered. 'I have the addresses, señora.'

'Will you give them to the inspector.'

He carelessly handed Alvarez a sheet of paper, turned to leave.

'One minute. Inspector, would you like another drink?'

'It is a thirsty day, señora, so I would.'

Benavides bent forward to pick up Alvarez's glass. He said, in a whisper, abandoning politeness altogether, 'For you, every bloody day is thirsty.'

Alvarez drove along the bay road. Clouds sent shadows rippling along the mountains as they responded to the changing shapes of rock faces. He passed a building under construction in a field which had once been known for the quality of the artichokes it grew. Would building continue until the area became more suburbia than countryside? Development was the curse, prosperity the benefit, of the past fifty years.

He turned into Cami de Ferent, stopped in front of Ca'n Llop, a *caseta* which had recently been enlarged, as was evident from the different colour of some of the stonework. Houses were often known by the nickname of the present or past owner. Had one been a wolf in some form – money, possessions, women? At a guess, there were now two or three bedrooms, bathroom, sitting and dining rooms, kitchen; before there would have been three rooms, perhaps one or more with only shutters and no glass windows, no running water, a brick oven, a long drop. María was not there. He looked at his watch. To locate Raquel's home would take time.

As he drove, he considered Laura Ashton. She was one of those regrettably few women whom one instinctively accepted to be without wiles. With her, there would be no sly glances, no carefully timed downcast eyes, no attempt to draw attention while seemingly avoiding it; she would not assess a man by the depth of his pockets; loyalty and compassion marked her. Ashton had been a lucky man.

There was no one at his home, despite the time. He opened the sideboard, brought out a bottle of Fundador and a glass, fetched ice cubes in an ice bucket from the kitchen, sat.

Twelve minutes later, Jaime came through the entrada and into the sitting/dining room. 'I'm starving. Is grub ready?'

'No.'

'Why not?'

'No one else is here.'

'Dolores must be getting lunch.'

'She doesn't know that.'

Jaime sat, poured himself a brandy. 'A man works all hours of the day, denies himself any pleasure to make up for his wife's extravagances, and what are his thanks? She can't be bothered to cook him a meal when he wants it. I'll tell her what I think when she returns.'

'Shouldn't advise that.'

'I'm to starve? She does her job properly or there'll be trouble for her!' He had spoken sufficiently loudly to mask the sounds of Dolores' return.

'For what trouble must I prepare myself?' she asked as she entered the room.

He was startled. 'I didn't hear you.'

'How could you when you spoke so loudly, it seemed you were addressing the neighbours?'

'I was talking to Enrique.'

'He has become deaf?'

'Where have you been?'

'Out.'

'I can see that.'

'Then why ask?'

'Where have you been?'

'I have just answered you.'

'I mean . . . Look, I'm hungry.'

'Then you will eat well.'

'There's nothing to eat. I expected to come back to a meal.'

'A man's expectations are like moonbeams.'

'But . . . It's . . . It's . . .'

'You have something to say?'

Jaime drew in a deep breath. 'It's a wife's duty to have a meal ready.'

'Then having discussed my duties, let us examine yours. If a wife is not at home when her husband expects her to be, he should wonder why and worry – has she suddenly been taken ill and rushed to hospital? Did she go shopping and get run over as she crossed the roads? Could she have suffered a stroke? When she returns home, unharmed, he should express his gratitude and joy in order to reassure her that she is his life. How did you express your gratitude? By demanding to know why your lunch was not on the table. Your belly was far more important than me helping Natalia.'

'But you—'

'I have not finished. A husband may lack all feeling for his wife, regard her as a domestic slave to be ordered around, but that does not abolish his duty to maintain his house as his wife has a right to expect. How do you maintain this house? The kitchen fan has needed repairing for so long it has probably seized up; the upstairs needs repainting; one of the Butano bottles has been empty for a month; the sink is clearing far too slowly; part of the guttering at the back looks insecure, and above it a tile is missing; the orange tree has not been sprayed.

'A husband should share with his wife the duty to look after the children. Juan is learning to swim. How often have you taken him to the sports centre? Isabel wants to learn Mallorquin dancing. Have you taken her to any of the classes? Do you have a close interest in their school work and go with me to the parents' day at her school to speak to the masters?'

'I had to drive into Palma—'

'At the time, your excuse was that a great friend was ill and you'd promised to go to the hospital to cheer him up.'

'You've got things all mixed up.'

'It is your misfortune that I have a good memory. It is my misfortune that I believed it to be my duty to prepare a meal which could be served immediately on my return since this would please you.'

Jaime picked up the bottle to refill his glass.

'You have drunk enough.'

'I've only had one!'

'Your memory deteriorates by the minute.' She went through to the kitchen.

'She won't believe me even when I tell the truth,' he said bitterly.

THIRTEEN

Alvarez left the car and walked up the short path to the front door of Ca'n Llop. He opened the door, stepped inside, called out, a small dog barked. The stone walls of the *entrada* had been plastered, the floor was tiled, the sloping ceiling was beamed. On a small table was a vase in which was a bunch of roses.

María Patera entered, told the dog to be quiet, closed the door behind herself. Plainly featured, she was dressed in a frock which draped, rather than fitted her. He introduced himself, explained the reason for his visit.

'I know nothing, but will make much of it.' She smiled as she quoted a local saying.

Her smile erased the suggestion of bitterness which her face held when in repose, the consequence of the uneasy quality of living which life had given her.

They sat in the central room.

'You want to talk to me? First, you will have a drink? I have only the wine a friend makes and it is not from Rioja.' Another quick smile.

'What is better than the wine from a friend?'

She left, returned with an earthenware jug and two glasses, filled one glass, handed it to him.

He drank. Were an oenophile to describe it, tasting of soil would be his mildest comment.

'I'd like to hear how you got on with the señor and señora. Were they pleasant to you?'

'Before I went to work there, which I had to do because such jobs have become difficult to find – I was worried because they were foreigners. They would say, do this, why have you not done that? But the señor was kind – ask Manuel – and the señora speaks to me as if to a friend. Perhaps she is not a true foreigner.'

'Would you think they were happy together?'

'How could they not be, living in such a home?'

'Things can be difficult in a palace.'

'Until he became ill, what was there to worry them?'

'Perhaps the difference in their ages.'

'For them, there was none. I have seen them look at each other as a newly married man looks at his bride.'

'Did she have friends of her own age?'

'Many.'

'The señor never objected?'

'Why should he?'

'He might have worried she would become too friendly with one of the young men of around her own age.'

'You think she would have warmed another man's bed?'

'It happens.'

'You understand nothing. Had you seen her tears when the señor died, you would not suggest such an absurdity.'

'Do you remember a man was found dead in the bay at the beginning of the month?'

'You think I have the memory of a flea?'

'Did you read about the scar on his neck and how we hoped someone would identify him because of it?'

'Now you think I cannot read?'

Since she was only slightly older than he, that would have been possible; until quite recently, some people could only identify themselves with a thumbprint. 'Did you ever see the man with such a scar at Son Dragó?'

'No.' She went through to the kitchen, returned with a glass into which she poured wine for herself. 'You have asked Manuel and Felipe questions, so they told me. Now you ask me the same ones. Why?'

'They didn't tell you that the dead man left a notebook in which he'd written the address of Son Dragó? That means he perhaps knew someone there. Such a person might be able to help us learn who murdered him.'

'Murdered?'

'You did not know?'

'Manuel said that's what it was, but he knows more than any encyclopedia, so we listen, but do not believe. There is something more you wish to know?'

'I don't think so.'

'Then when you've finished the wine, you won't be staying.'

Home-made wine and a blunt dismissal – the old Mallorca.

He returned to his car, sat behind the wheel, stared through the windscreen. There might be time to have a word with Raquel, but little annoyed Dolores so much as being late for a meal, even though that was quite normal for others.

The next day, Alvarez stepped into the hall of Son Dragó, returned Benavides' greeting, said: 'Is Raquel working here today?'

'Yes,' Benavides curtly answered.

He was glad other people had to work during a weekend. 'Will it be OK to have a word with her in the staff sitting-room?'

'I have been asked by the señora to give you all the help I can.' It was an obligation which Benavides obviously resented.

Five minutes later, Raquel walked into the room. Alvarez tried to conceal his surprise. She was in her early twenties, blonde, attractively featured, and enjoyed a body that must annoy most women. 'I'm sorry to drag you away from your work.'

'Do that whenever you like,' she answered.

Her smile revealed regular, white teeth. Without being able to explain why, he gained the impression she was of an ardent nature.

'Manuel said you'd want to ask me about the man who drowned.'

Her tone had changed and suggested she could have mistaken his admiration for prurience.

'I'm trying to find out if he ever called here.'

'Not as far as I know.'

'No one has casually mentioned seeing him somewhere about the estate?'

'Why ask me? You've spoken to the others, so if they had seen him, they would have told you.'

She had begun to annoy him. 'I have to make absolutely certain of the facts.'

'Is there anything more you want to know?'

'Not for the moment.'

He watched her leave. A shining red pimiento looked attractive, but it would bite the tongue.

There was a gentle knock on the door. He called out to enter. Inés took a half-step into the room, came to a stop.

'Hullo! How are things going?' he asked. She was nervous, even frightened, he judged. 'Is there some way I can help you?'

She stared down at the floor.

'Come on in and sit.'

Almost a minute passed before she finally did so. Seated, she gripped her hands tightly together.

'Are you troubled about something, Inés?' he asked quietly.

She nodded.

'Is it a very difficult trouble?'

She nodded again.

'Tell me what is the matter so that I can help you.'

'My dad—' She stopped.

Physical or mental assault? Domestic violence had become much more frequent or, if one were a cynic, more frequently reported. 'Whatever you say to me won't go beyond these walls.'

She looked directly at him, then hurriedly away.

The door opened, and Benavides entered. 'Please excuse this intrusion, inspector, but I wondered where Inés was. Beatriz needs help in the kitchen.'

'I'm afraid she'll have to wait. I want a word with Inés.'

'Then I'll stay.'

'Why?'

'As I explained previously, I try to give her support.'

He would have agreed to the request, had he not noticed Ines' expression. 'I don't think that will be necessary.'

'What do you want to ask her?'

'I am not yet certain.'

'Then I really should remain.'

'If she wants to leave, she may; if she stays, but becomes distressed, I'll call you.'

'As you say, inspector,' Benavides said angrily. He spoke to Inés. 'Don't forget.'

'What is she to remember?' Alvarez asked sharply.

'To help Beatriz as soon as she leaves here.'

'I'll remind her.'

Benavides left.

'It's a pity we were interrupted,' Alvarez said, 'but he was trying to help you, wasn't he?'

She said nothing.

'Are you unhappy at home?'

He waited. 'Inés, we all have problems we find terribly difficult to talk about, so I'll ask you a few questions and you can answer them very briefly. Am I right in thinking that what you said before Manuel came in here means your trouble is what happens at home?'

'He . . . he's . . .'

'Does your father do things which embarrass you?'

She rushed her words. 'He won't let me wear clothes like the others do because he says they look indecent. He won't let me go out with friends in the evening because that leads to mortal sin.'

A father who perhaps remembered too much about his youth. 'Is that why you're so unhappy?'

'Yes, but . . . That is . . .'

'Tell me.'

She stared at her feet.

'If you tell me what it is that so worries you, I may be able to help.'

She seemed to take a deep breath before she said: 'He says that if I ever lie, I'll go straight to hell.'

'If that were so, I don't think there would be many people in heaven.'

'It's better to be deaf, dumb and blind than to lie and be cast into hell's fires. I don't want to be blind.'

'You have lied?'

After a while, she nodded.

'About what?'

'I . . . I said I hadn't seen him.' Her voice had become shrill.

'You have a boyfriend and your father doesn't like him?'

'It was a terrible lie. I did see him. I knew it was him because of the scar.'

In his mind there was a clap of mental thunder. Facts form a theory, a theory must never form facts. Because he had theorized that she suffered parental trouble, he had presumed . . . 'You saw Kerr, the man who died in the bay?'

It was several seconds before she nodded.

'When?'

'He said I mustn't tell anyone about it.'

'Kerr said that?'

'Manuel.'

'Did he say why?'

She ignored the question. 'It was a terrible lie. I was scared, and last night I dreamt I was made to walk towards a huge flame and my father was laughing. A dream says what's going to happen.'

'It is the most useless prophet there's ever been. Last week, I dreamt my *decimo* had won. When I woke up, I thought of all that I'd do with the money. At the lottery shop, I found I'd won nothing.'

'But my dream means—'

'That you had been worrying about what your father had said to you, nothing more. You must often dream?'

She nodded.

'Has a single one of those dreams come true?'

After a moment, she shook her head.

'Neither will this one.'

'You really think that?'

'I know it for certain.'

He waited, then asked: 'When did you meet Kerr?'

'I . . . can't remember.'

'Was it when the almonds were in blossom, the grapes were forming, or the oranges were being harvested?'

'It was . . . just before Elena's birthday party. I wasn't allowed to go because parties lead to sin.'

'When does she have a birthday?'

'September the twenty-fourth,' she answered immediately.

'And where were you?'

'Here. Manuel was busy, and Beatriz was in bed. She had some kind of bug which a lot of people were catching.'

'You go to answer to the front door if no one else can. Is that what happened?'

'He wasn't like the people who usually come here. He hadn't shaved.'

Alvarez was gratified that he had remembered to shave that morning. 'What did he want?'

'He couldn't speak Spanish and I know hardly any English, although the señora tries to help me learn some. He kept saying the señora's name, so I said she and the señor had gone out. Manuel came and told the man to clear off, and eventually he left.'

'Did he tell you his name?'

She shook her head.

'Tell me how you can be certain who he was?'

'He had the scar.'

'You had read about the man who died in the bay and the description of the scar on his neck?'

'But when I told Manuel what I'd realized, he said I was talking nonsense. He couldn't have been the man who died in the bay.'

'Did you accept you might have been mistaken?'

'I kept telling him, I knew it was that man. In the end, Manuel said if it was him, it would cause the señora so much trouble if it was known he'd come to speak to her that I must forget about it. That's why I . . . I lied to you.'

'You did not lie.'

'I told you I hadn't seen him, but I had.'

'Do you know why people lie?'

She did not answer.

'It is to make someone believe something that's not true. If that person doesn't believe what he's been told, what was said becomes meaningless and there has not been a lie. You have told me what did happen, I have not been deceived, you have not lied.'

She fiddled with the button on her frock. 'I . . . I won't go to hell?'

'Neither now, or at any other time.'

'I've been so . . . so frightened.'

'Forget your fears.'

'But I'll have to confess to Dad and he'll—'

'I've just explained why you have not lied, so you do not have any reason to confess about anything.'

She was silent for almost a minute, then said: 'You won't tell Manuel what I've said to you, will you, or he'll be so angry. He'll tell the señora I don't do the work properly. He didn't want me to come here, but the señora asked me about my family and said I was to work here.'

'He'll not know you've told me anything.'

She looked far less tense when she left.

Alvarez was not surprised when Benavides knocked on the door, stepped inside and asked: 'Is everything in order, inspector?'

'As right as it ever is.'

'Inés was not too confused?'

'I understood everything she told me.'

'Was she able to help you?'

'Only in a negative sense. She corroborated what she'd said before.'

'Then she really can't assist you?'

'She seems to lead a very strict life.'

'Her father belongs to a strange religious society.'

'Hot on fires.'

'I beg your pardon?'

'A meaningless comment.'

The television programme came to an end. Dolores stood, went over to the set.

'Don't switch off,' Jaime said.

'You intend to continue watching when it is time for bed?'

'The next programme could be interesting.'

'On this channel, it is a study of buffalo in America over the past two hundred years. Perhaps, when I am in bed, you intend to change channels to watch the film which is being shown and is described as inflammatory. You are interested in firefighting?'

'You always misjudge me.'

'As my mother used to say, a man's mind is a mansion for

one subject and a shoe cupboard for all others.' She climbed the stairs and went into the bedroom, closed the door forcefully.

'Why didn't you say something?' Jaime demanded.

'About what?' Alvarez asked.

'Her making out we wanted to watch the film because it's hot.'

'You think she hadn't seen the photograph in the telly magazine of a woman having a shower behind semi-transparent shower curtains?'

'There was no need for her to think that's why *I* want to see the film.'

'The fires of hell are singeing you.'

'What's that supposed to mean?'

'Great perils lie in wait for lying mortals.'

'Have you been drinking since lunch?'

'I have not had that pleasure.'

'Then what's got you talking daft?'

'An insoluble problem.'

'How to persuade her your hand was reaching for the gear lever?'

'How to reconcile an unbreakable promise not to do something while doing it.'

'You'd run circles backwards.'

Jaime had a point, Alvarez accepted. What could have persuaded him to promise Inés to do the impossible?

He awoke, yawned, allowed himself another five minutes before he got up and dressed, went downstairs to the kitchen. Dolores was seated at the table, reading a book. She looked up. 'You are not going to work this morning?'

'It's Sunday, so there's no rush. It does one good to take things easily.'

'You have the experience of doing anything else?'

She was in one of her moods, he thought. 'Is the chocolate made?'

'It will need reheating since I had forgotten you and Jaime spent the night watching a green film which disgraced both those who acted in it and those who watched it.'

'It wasn't like that. There was just the one very quick scene; the photo of it was in the programme magazine.'

'If true, that is the explanation of my husband's ill humour when he finally came to bed. Perhaps, like you, he continued to watch in case your misguided hopes were finally met.'

He tried to lighten the atmosphere. 'Is that a cookery book you're reading?'

'Since the cover is a photo of *Lomos de bacalao fresco con champiñones*, it seems possible.'

'Are you thinking of cooking that?'

'It had not occurred to me.'

'Prepared by you, it would be ambrosia.'

'That is probable.'

'Then perhaps?'

'When you are both not too tired to know what you are eating because of an ill-spent night, I might consider it.'

The wise man evaded trouble. 'I'd better start moving.'

'You are suddenly in a rush?'

'There's a lot going on at work. Perhaps it will help if I heat the chocolate?'

'When you will have the gas so high, the chocolate will boil?' She closed the book, crossed to a working surface and picked up a saucepan, lit a gas ring, reduced the flame to the minimum.

'I don't expect you had time to buy some *ensaimadas*?' he unwisely asked.

'You are correct. Were I two people, I should still not have enough time to do what is expected of me.'

'Hopefully there are some biscuits?'

'Do I maintain so poor a home that there are likely to be none?'

He said nothing. The old soldier's advice still held good. When the bullets buzz, stay under the parapet.

The phone rang soon after he entered his office.

'Roberto here,' Plá said. 'There's a drowned elephant in the bay.'

'Swim out and pull it ashore.'

'I can't swim.'

'Don't let that stop you trying.'

'No sense of humour? Or do you only find it funny when someone else suffers?'

'Unless you've a reason for phoning, I'm busy.'

'A touch of the superior chief? You know Sacar La Moda down on the front?'

'No.'

'Every time you pass the shop, you look at the scanty underwear on show and hope you'll have the fortune to meet someone wearing it.'

'You've the mind of a schoolboy.'

'Which is why we gain pleasure in each other's company. Half an hour ago, a woman went into the shop and started looking at frocks after placing her handbag on the counter. She finally decided to try on a frock, went into the changing room and the assistant followed to tell her how ravishingly beautiful she looked in it. A man entered, grabbed the handbag and ran. The victim says there were over two hundred euros in the handbag.'

'Had she just been to a bank to withdraw cash?'

'How would I know?'

'By asking her. Then you can find out if she's fudging the amount for a better insurance payout.'

'Do you believe anyone?'

'Myself.'

'Then you're being conned. Does the manner of the robbery tell you anything?'

'That women shouldn't leave their handbags on a counter.'

'If you'd been called to console the victim, she'd have ended up hysterical. What about names of likely thieves?'

'Can't think of any offhand.'

'You must have had dozens of similar cases.'

'Not when they're policía work.'

'When they get serious, they're Cuerpo's.'

'Call me when another half dozen women have lost their bags.'

'I'm damned if I know why I thought you might help.'

Alvarez raised his arm to look at his watch. It would be advisable to wait another half hour before returning home for supper. It was to be hoped that Dolores had overcome her irritable belief that Jaime and he had been watching a green film the previous night; in the traditional sense, it had been soft pornography. The reasonable criticism would be that the plot was very familiar. A poor young woman, an ailing father who needed unaffordable medical attention, a doctor who promised to help when he and she became close friends, seduction poorly represented, desertion by the doctor, the beginning of a downward life spiral for the young woman suddenly halted when she met a rich, older man, happiness at last, reappearance of the doctor and the demand of much money to keep her secret secret.

He lit a cigarette and his thoughts returned to the case. Did he accept Inés' evidence? If true, the fact had been concealed by the staff in a conspiracy of silence. Why? A question which had to be answered.

Benavides had tried to frighten Inés into silence by the threat she would lose her job. She was aware that she might find it difficult, even impossible, to find another home where the señora would employ her from a sense of sympathy. If he demanded Benavides told him why he had threatened her, it would be obvious she had told him. The señora, deep in sorrow, could not be expected to ignore Benavides' advice a second time.

He brought a bottle of Terry brandy and a glass out of the bottom drawer of the desk. Alcohol might not, in truth, sharpen the mind, but it allowed one to forget how blunt it could be. He lit another cigarette. Could he say he'd been told by someone, unconnected to Inés, that he had seen Kerr visit the house? A casual trespasser in the garden who had chanced to see Kerr . . .? But why would Manuel have noticed him? How had this trespasser informed the Cuerpo? Why should a casual visitor mention having seen Kerr?

His duty was clear. Honour the demands of his work, accept there was no room for emotion. He must inform Salas of the new evidence after he had questioned Benavides, even though Inés must suffer, if not through losing her job – an appeal to the señora not to dismiss her? – but from the hostility of the other members of staff. When one had to face alternative courses of action, both of which were wrong, how to judge which one to take? The young woman in the previous night's film had known she should preserve her honour, but not to do so would save her father's life . . . unhappiness . . . marriage to a wealthy man restoring happiness . . . her seducer black-mailing her . . .

Blackmail? Over what?

He poured himself another drink.

FOURTEEN

Benavides opened the front door, his welcoming smile as false as ever. 'A pleasant evening, inspector, but the wind has the hint of approaching winter.'

'Probably. I want a word with Señora Ashton.'

'She is sailing. I regret I cannot say when she will return.'

'Is she on her own?'

'Yes.'

'García not with her?'

'She should have no need of the engines because of the direction and constancy of the wind.'

Sailing on her own to dim memories or, perversely, evoke them, as some in bitter despair might do? 'Does she know what she's doing in a yacht?'

'The señor said that she held as good a helm as he did. Can I assist you, inspector?'

'By having a word.'

'If you would like to enter?'

They went through to the staff sitting-room.

'Please sit, inspector.'

What was hidden behind those plummy, obsequious words, Alvarez wondered. Contempt? Staff – not from the island – often assumed their employers' social standing, and an ill-dressed police officer enjoyed no status. Had Benavides been a Mallorquin, he would have understood that wealth was a measure only of wealth, social standing was a figment of imagination. 'I had a chat with Inés yesterday evening.'

'I remember.'

'As I said, she merely confirmed what she had told me before.'

'As you will have understood, inspector, she has an unfortunate home life which affects her level of intelligence.'

Inés was almost cleared of grassing. Now to learn whether Benavides would withstand a direct attack. 'You know you inherit a bequest under Señor Ashton's will?'

Benavides was briefly hazed by the change of subject. 'The señora has mentioned this,' he finally answered.

'Ten thousand euros. A generous gift from a generous employer.'

'Indeed.'

'Much as you'd expected?'

'There was no reason to be remembered in the señor's will.'

'Even though servants whose services were appreciated often are?'

'One enters service to serve, not in the hopes of a legacy.'

'After years in the home of a rich man, it would be unusual not to wonder if there will be one when illness suggests death cannot be far away.'

'My concern was for the señor, nothing else.'

'Is a copy of his will in the house?'

'I cannot say.'

'Is there a safe?'

'In the library.'

'The copy of it is probably in that. Does the safe have a combination lock?'

'No.'

'So where did the señor keep the keys?'

'I cannot say.'

'Unfortunate, if you wanted to look inside the safe and read the will when the señor and señora were out.'

'You have no right to make so slanderous and unfounded a suggestion.'

'My superior chief says crime and money are like a hen and an egg. You don't get one without the other. It must have been very frustrating not to know where the keys were, not to be able to open the will and read what you would receive.'

Benavides stood. Anger altered the pitch of his voice. 'I will not stay to listen to your contemptible inferences.'

'Why did you not call the police after Kerr came to the house?'

He stared at Alvarez, fear beginning to mark his plump face. 'That is ridiculous. I never saw him, could not have met him. Are you relying on something Inés told you? If so, it was imagination.'

'She said nothing concerning Kerr.'

'Then why do you suggest I met the man?'

'It wouldn't have occurred to me to do so until I learned from England that he had a criminal background,' Alvarez lied. 'Then, it became obvious. You made contact because you wanted the safe opened.'

'How could I know he was a crook?' Benavides asked hoarsely.

'A good question. I hope we'll have the answer before you go on trial.'

'Trial? In God's name, trial for what?'

'Murdering Kerr because he blackmailed you by threatening to expose you. That so frightened you, you failed to realize his threat had to be a bluff because if he exposed you, he must incriminate himself.'

Benavides ran a finger around the neck of his shirt, as if it were causing breathing problems. 'I swear that's crazy. I never met Kerr . . .'

'The staff have denied with considerable force that they had never seen or heard of Kerr before his death. I've tried to think why they should all be so emphatic and wondered if you had ordered them, if asked by me, to deny the possibility. I asked myself, why would you do that without very good cause? The answer was clear. You were incriminated in Kerr's murder.'

Benavides made a sound resembling a sob as he produced a handkerchief and, with shaking hands, wiped the sweat from his face.

Alvarez waited for the other to regain a measure of emotional control. Then he would repeat that Inés had not mentioned Kerr to him and it was only . . .

'I did that to save the señora,' Benavides said wildly.

'From what?'

'People believing she could have any reason to kill Kerr.'

'She is the main beneficiary under the will.'

'It's nothing to do with that.'

Alvarez's thoughts became bitter. Like the young woman in the film, his attempt to help Inés seemed it might lead to disastrous consequences. 'Then why should she become suspect?'

'Christ, I need a drink!' Benavides ran out of the room.

Alvarez's need for one was as great, but he doubted that in the chaos of his mind, Benavides would remember his duty as a butler and bring him one. Why should anyone believe it possible she could have murdered Kerr if her inheritance was not involved?

Benavides, a glass in one hand, returned, sat.

'Why should the police believe Señora Ashton was responsible for Kerr's death?'

'The phone calls.' He drank deeply, half emptying the glass.

'Tell me about them.'

'The first was when I was on holiday, and Inés answered. She told me what had happened. I didn't believe her and thought it was one of her stories. Then Beatriz told me that after the call, the señora had become so disturbed, the señor became worried she was ill. The doctor could find nothing physically wrong with her.'

'Go back to the beginning. You were away, Inés answered the phone. A man spoke in English so she couldn't understand him, but she realized he wanted to speak to the señora. She took the call, which knocked her sideways. Did you learn why the call had so disturbed her?'

'The next day there was another, and I answered it. A man said in English, which I could just understand, that he wished to speak to Señora Ashton. I asked for his name, and he said it was Kerr. I informed the señora, and she was terrified.'

'What made you think that?'

'The way she looked, said to tell the caller she had gone out.'

'So she didn't answer the call?'

'She did another time.'

'Which was when?'

'She was having tea on her own because the señor was sailing. It was Kerr again. I returned to the sitting room and told the señora, who tried very hard not to seem upset, but she did not lift the receiver until I had left. I went back to the hall to replace the receiver in the hall.'

'And heard?'

'Inspector, I was very worried. She was frightened. I knew

the caller had to be a threat to her, and I had to know if I could help.'

'What did you hear?'

'Kerr told her he wanted the money, or else.'

'Or else what?'

'He did not say.'

'How did she respond to the threat?'

'Said she would try to get it for him and pleaded with him not to do anything. He said he wouldn't wait for long. That was all.'

'Did Kerr come to the house?'

'Later on.'

'Give me the facts.'

'I heard a man talking to Inés and went to find out what was happening because she can say and do awkward things when she doesn't know someone and is nervous. He was telling her he wanted to speak to the señora. I was certain I recognized the voice of the man who'd phoned and whose name had so disturbed the señora. The señor was not at home, so I told the man to clear off. It was only when the photos and drawings were in the papers and on the television that I realized Kerr was the man who'd been found, murdered, in the bay.

'I knew that if it became known he had phoned, terrified her, had called at the house, it was inevitable people would start to think she must be guilty. So I told the staff to forget everything.'

'Do you believe Señora Ashton killed Kerr?'

'Of course I don't,' he answered violently. 'Can't you understand, don't you realize what kind of a person she is?'

'People wear masks.'

'If she smiles, she's happy; if something unpleasant happens, even if it doesn't concern her, she's unhappy and tries to help. No one else would have employed Inés. To my shame, I knew the trouble she had at home with her father, but I said to the señor she should not work here because he entertained many important people who might be disturbed by her. He would have accepted my advice, but the señora said she must be helped and she was to be employed.'

'Further reason to admire the señora.'

'I tell you, she could have had no part in Kerr's murder.'

'You are a stout friend.'

'I would not make the mistake of calling her a friend. But she could not be more friendly.' Benavides moved uneasily. 'You will have to speak to her about Kerr?'

'It is now impossible not to do so.'

'Because of what I told you.' He spoke bitterly. 'I should have let you believe I murdered Kerr rather than give you cause to think she could have done.'

A noble sentiment, easily spoken, Alvarez thought.

'Señor,' he said over the phone the next morning. 'I have uncovered fresh facts in the case concerning the murder of Kerr.'

'What are they?' Salas asked curtly.

'I have spoken at length to Manuel Benavides, the butler at Son Dragó. Kerr phoned Señora Ashton more than once, each call causing her great distress.'

'Do you know the times and dates of these calls?'

'No. Benavides could not remember sufficiently accurately for me to enter them.'

'Into what did you not enter them? What are you trying to tell me?'

'Because Benavides could not remember dates and times with any accuracy, I did not enter them in my log.'

'Did Señora Ashton report these calls to you?'

'No, señor.'

'And you unfortunately forgot about them until now?'

'I have only just learned of them.'

'They were made before Kerr was identified.'

'He could hardly have phoned after he was dead.'

'It escapes you that I was confirming something which you might well have overlooked? Before the dead man was identified, there was no reason for anyone who had known Kerr to report the fact.'

'No, señor.'

'You do not find that obvious?'

'I was saying that it had not escaped my mind. Had I said "Yes" you might have thought I was agreeing it had done so. It's the problem of—'

'A problem only to someone such as you. Have you anything more to tell me?'

'As I said—'

'Do not repeat yourself.'

'Her husband thought she was physically ill.'

'Is it possible to relate what you have just said to what you have earlier mentioned?'

'She was so distressed by the phone calls that her husband thought she was ill and called the doctor.'

'Might it not have seemed reasonable to have explained that originally?'

'You told me not to repeat myself.'

'I will speak as simply as possible, and you will try to concentrate, so that there is the possibility, however remote, that I will have a rough idea of what you have been saying. Did you learn why the telephone calls so disturbed Señora Ashton?'

'Inés answered the first one. She is what I suppose one would call a general factotum, who—'

'You may accept that I am well aware of her position.'

'She speaks so little English, she couldn't understand the man, but since he kept saying the señora's name, she told the señora, who, Ines said, was obviously greatly disturbed. The next day, Benavides answered a second call from Kerr. When he told the señora who was calling, she was terrified and would not speak to the caller. The third time, she did. Because he needed to replace the receiver of his phone, he heard, by chance, what was being said. Kerr was demanding money and threatening the señora if he did not receive it.'

'Demanding on what grounds?'

'Benavides was unable to learn.'

'Even though he was listening on another phone, as is to be expected from a Mallorquin.'

'He comes from Valladolid.'

'One or both of his parents will have come from this island.'

'Some time after the phone calls, when the señor was out in his yacht, Kerr visited Son Dragó. Inés opened the front door. Benavides, who can speak some English, heard Kerr

talking and went into the hall and asked the newcomer what
he wanted. Benavides became convinced from the way the
man spoke that he had made the phone calls which had so
disturbed the señora. He told him to clear off. Kerr left.'

'You have questioned Señora Ashton?'

'No.'

'Why not? You now know she was threatened over the
phone and was visited by Kerr. Even you should be able to
comprehend that it is essential to question her in order to
uncover the truth.'

'But if it's not how it seems and can be explained . . .'

'How do you explain a threat of blackmail?'

'As I mentioned, Benavides speaks some English, but is far
from fluent. There's the chance he muddled up what Kerr said,
both on the phone and—'

'You have not expressed any such doubt until now.'

'When listening to the conversation on the phone, he would
have been worried he might be caught, and when under tension,
one's memory can become unreliable.'

'You are frequently under tension?'

'Why do you suggest that, señor?'

'You have forgotten the four thousand two hundred euros
found in Kerr's possession. By the laws of probability, they were
paid in response to the demand made over the telephone.'

'You have always made the point that that is a possibility,
not a fact.'

'It would help if you could appreciate that different circumstances affect facts.'

'Surely a fact is a fact?'

'I was forgetting the necessity to explain matters to you in
a simple form. Circumstances can change the light in which
facts are viewed.'

'The euros were withdrawn by the señor, not the señora.'

'You find it difficult to understand that a husband will defend
his wife to the utmost of his ability?'

'But—'

'You will tell the señora you have proof she was being
blackmailed, and you will demand what provided the cause
for this.'

'If you're beginning to think she could have had a hand in Kerr's murder . . .'

'A possibility which became a probability the moment the link between Kerr and the Ashtons was established.'

'One could make the mistake of thinking she might in some way be involved in the murder, but that is totally to ignore the kind of person she is.'

'I know of no one whose judgement of character should carry less weight than yours. Report to me when you have questioned her.'

FIFTEEN

Greixonera de senyals: lamb fries, olive oil, lemon juice, lard, eggs, milk, flour, breadcrumbs, nutmeg, pepper and salt. Dolores had added culinary magic to the marinated fries. Alvarez was slightly annoyed when Juan and Isabel demanded second helpings before leaving the table. His second helping thus became smaller.

'I should like to go to Mestara,' she said.

There was no response.

'Cristina is fortunate. Luis is happy to drive her to wherever she wishes to go.'

'Because if he doesn't, she forgets to buy what he likes,' Jaime muttered.

'How do you know that?'

'Luis told me.'

'Interesting!'

Alvarez wondered how long it would be before Jaime understood the unspoken threat.

'I suppose I could go by bus, but then it is impossible to carry anything heavy.'

Such as wine. 'One of us should be able to drive you.'

'I would not wish either of you to disturb yourself in order to do so.' The false wish was sweetly spoken. She carried plates and cutlery into the kitchen.

Alvarez refilled his glass, leaned forward. 'Why tell her that?' he asked in a very low voice.

'Tell her what?' Jaime asked.

'Cristina cuts off his wine if he doesn't take her shopping.'

'She didn't say that's what would happen to us. She would never do something as rotten as that.'

'Why d'you think she remarked it was interesting news?'

Jaime refilled his glass after a quick look to see she was not watching him from the kitchen. 'You think she could be wondering about trying that with us?'

'Without a moment's hesitation.'

'Then I'll make it clear she can forget it.'

'And she'll tell us to buy our own booze.'

'A husband made to do the shopping? Never!'

'Women's liberation means attempted female domination.'

'You think she'll ever get the chance to dominate me?'

'It's not impossible.'

'Next thing, women will start reckoning they're as good as men at everything.'

'Not when it comes to having babies.'

'It's no good talking to you when you're in one of your daft moods. I suppose that's because you've made a balls-up at work.'

'In one sense, you could say that.'

Dolores stepped through the bead curtain. 'If you wish to continue talking about things you do not wish me to know about, I'll have my orange in the kitchen.'

'We were only saying—' Jaime began.

Alvarez hastily intervened. 'That we don't understand how a woman can prepare wonderful meals, keep a house spotlessly clean, and then go out of her way to help others.'

'If I was a naive fifteen, I might find your words flattering.' She returned to the kitchen, reappeared with a bowl of oranges, three plates, and three small steel knives.

'It need not be until tomorrow,' she said as she sat.

'What needn't?' Jaime asked.

'That one of you drives me to Mestara.'

'I would happily do so,' Alvarez said, 'if only the case I'm on hadn't become so complicated, and the superior chief so impatient, that I have to spend twelve hours a day at work.'

'Twelve?' she said, expressing surprise. 'Are you sure that's correct when you have an hour for breakfast, two hours at lunch, a siesta of two to three hours, after supper a couple of hours watching a film of an obnoxious nature, and finally a sleep of very many hours?'

'If I do have a siesta today, it will be a very short one. I have to question a woman, and I don't know how to go about it.'

'Try speaking to her,' Jaime suggested.

'This woman is English?' she asked.

'Yes,' Alvarez replied.

'Young?'

'Youngish.'

'Beautiful?'

'Even if she was visually perfect, even though she is now so wealthy she could light cigarettes with hundred euro notes, I am not romantically interested in her.'

'You are quick to deny something which has not been said.'

'Maybe she's not ¡*Hola!* material, but the money will make up for that,' Jaime observed.

'She is newly bereaved.'

'Very ready to be comforted.'

'You hold marriage to be of as little account to a woman as it is to a man?' she asked Jaime sharply. 'Money is of far greater importance than affection. You cannot understand why someone who has lost a beloved wife or husband is too bereaved to think of another relationship. Perhaps I can be thankful for your sake that if I die first, you will suffer no sorrow since you will no longer have the cost of feeding me.'

'What are you going on about? If you die before me, I'll be inconsolable.'

'Because you will no longer get your meals cooked, the house cleaned, your clothes washed and ironed, a shoulder to lean on when something insignificant upsets you. But perhaps you will die first, content in the knowledge I will tend your grave every day with fresh flowers and through the distorted glass of memory will remember you as a man of love, compassion, and great kindness.' She stood. 'I will go up to my bedroom. If you want coffee, you will make it.'

They watched her climb the stairs and turn into the passage; a door was shut.

'If you had four feet,' Alvarez said, 'you'd put them all in your mouth at the same time.'

'I suppose you think that's amusing?'

'With her in an ill temper and supper to cook, and me being told to believe the impossible, there is not a sliver of humour in my universe.'

Alvarez's customary pleasure gained from driving along the bay road was absent. His mind was too occupied with the coming meeting, his need to question Señora Ashton and inevitably making it seem he believed her capable of, guilty of, murdering Kerr . . .

As Alvarez drew up outside Son Dragó, Benavides stepped out through the front doorway, walked over to the car. 'You wish to speak to me again?'

'No. With the señora.'

'She is not here.'

There was a call from the hall. 'Manuel?'

'She has a sister who sounds exactly like her?' Alvarez asked sarcastically.

'Inspector, please forget what I told you.' Emotional pain was visible in the expression on his plump face. 'She can't have done it.'

'Emilio,' Laura said as they entered the hall, 'I want to know if you can tell me . . . Inspector!'

'Good evening, señora.'

'You're working late.'

'Unfortunately so.'

'Whom do you wish to talk to this time?'

'You, señora.'

'You'll find it a fruitless conversation.'

'I sincerely hope so, señora.'

'A strange wish.' She looked quizzically at him. 'We'll go into the sitting room.'

Benavides crossed the tiled floor, opened the door, stood to one side as they entered.

'Inspector, would you like coffee or a drink?' she asked as she sat.

'If I might have a drink.'

She spoke to Benavides. 'I'll have an orange juice.'

He left the room.

'May I ask you an out-of-the-way question?' she asked Alvarez.

'Of course, señora.'

'You must notice more about people than most. Do you think Manuel is very troubled about something?'

'I wouldn't have judged so.'

'I've gained the impression he has become reluctant to stay here because, bluntly, I am now his employer.'

Benavides saw himself as a traitor and was ashamed to face the woman he had betrayed. 'Señora, I am as certain as I can be that your fears are unjustified. He has told me how happy he is to serve you, as he did your husband.'

'Thank you for telling me. Now, an impertinent question.' Again, that artless smile which escaped her sadness. 'Have you always lived in Mallorca?'

'I was born at the other end of the island and was there for many years before I moved to this end.'

'You must have seen many changes.'

'So many, I sometimes wonder if I remember correctly.'

'A friend who has been here for a long time says it's been like moving a century in forty years.'

'In some ways, he is correct. When he first came to the island, it is likely roads were badly made, were dirt in villages; shops were family run and sold mainly locally produced food; the furniture was limited; towns had irregular electricity and in the countryside there was often none; as little as two hectares of land would enable a man to grow the food his family needed; donkey carts were the major form of travel; doctors were few, and many patients could not afford their fees, yet perhaps were treated for nothing; and pigs were killed at *matançes* and might provide the only meat a family would eat for a long while. When tourists arrived and brought money with them, goods were imported from abroad and for a while could become a symbol of pride. Refrigerators were kept in the *entrada* so that friends and neighbours would see them, cars became commonplace, roads were macadamized, donkey carts became too dangerous to be used in the growing traffic, and super-markets introduced food and goods from around the world.'

'It was a wonderful change for people?'

'We used to have a saying, señora. Find a hundred peseta coin and tomorrow you will receive a bill for a hundred and one pesetas. When there were few rich but many peasants, peasants envied only the rich. As times changed, the man with a Seat Punto envied the man with a Mercedes, and the owner

of a small town house envied the owner of a large villa in
one of the *urbanizacións*. Drug dependancy arrived and, with
it, theft in order to sustain the dependency. Houses had to be
locked. Supermarkets drove the small family-run shops out of
business. Land began to lie idle because to work it demanded
too much labour for too little income.'

'Then modernization was a bad thing?'

'There are now doctors and health centres in every town or
large village, hospitals treat the ill without payment, and no rich
man can use the threat of poverty to make another do as he
demands. It is like an orange tree. Never feed and water it and
it will produce small, juiceless oranges; feed and water it too
heavily and the oranges will be large, but will have less taste
and begin to rot soon after picking.'

'One needs the happy medium.'

'But how does one know what that is until one has learned
what it is not?'

There was a knock on the door, and Benavides entered. He
straightened the runner on Laura's table, placed the glass of
orange juice on it; as he handed Alvarez a brandy and ice,
he mouthed a few words. He was no lip-reader, yet Alvarez
was convinced he had been asked to ignore what he had
learned.

Laura held the glass above her lap. 'It's been interesting
to talk to you, but I'm sure you're wanting to ask more
questions.'

'I fear so.'

'Then let's get them over and done with.'

'Señora . . .'

'Yes?'

'It is difficult for me.'

She smiled. 'And for me as I wait to answer a question
which might be about anything.'

'Is it correct that you knew Colin Kerr?'

She started, as if jabbed by a needle; the features of her
face tightened, and a smile was aeons away. She had forgotten
the glass in her hand, and it tilted to spill orange juice over
her dress. She stood, hurried out of the room.

He stared through the nearer window at the bay. Shock or

surprise? Surprise because she had believed any such contact was unknown or shock because this had been disclosed?

If Kerr had been blackmailing her, over what?

Benavides entered, spoke angrily. 'The señora says it will take time to change, so you can leave.'

Alvarez sat in his office, stared through the unshuttered window at the uninviting view of the wall of the property on the other side of the road. Had Benavides merely blamed him for the accident of the orange juice, or had he feared a continued questioning of the señora could uncover a new link to inculpate her and that was why, in the señora's name, he had been told to get out? Was Benavides constantly, by word and manner, denying the possibility of her guilt in order to cover his own guilt? Would it be a waste of time further to consider the possibility of a link between Kerr's death and the staff? Salas had contemptuously dismissed the possibility that Kerr had a criminal record in England, but was that possibility so absurd? A further request to ask for the information to be provided would be sharply dismissed since Salas viewed hunches as pernicious irrelevancies. What would be the consequences to him if Salas was right and he was wrong?

He opened a top drawer of the desk and brought out a list of the telephone numbers of international police forces.

He hoped Salas had been called away to a meeting, was in conference, had slipped out for a quick drink, even fallen when crossing a road to be overwhelmed by a bus. Hope was the drug of mankind.

'Yes?' Salas said.

'Inspector Alvarez speaking.'

'I am aware of that.'

'I mentioned my name because in the past you have said—'

'That I am too busy to suffer my time being wasted. You have something to report?'

'I began to question Señora Ashton as you unfortunately demanded.'

'Why unfortunately? Why *began* yet seemingly did not finish?'

'She became upset and spilled a glass of orange juice over her dress and had to leave to change. She sent Benavides to tell me this would take a long time and so I should go.'

'You believed her?'

'I had no option.'

'You are unaware how quickly a woman can change a dress?'

'Yes, señor.'

'I should like to believe that, but cannot. Did you shout at her as if she was a fishwife?'

'No, señor. I began by telling her a little about the local history . . .'

'Quite unnecessary and uninteresting. Your questioning was inconclusive?'

'I wouldn't say that, when it seemed possible she was acknowledging she had known Kerr.'

'In what way?'

'It's possible she was so shocked when I asked her if it was correct she knew Kerr that she started and consequently spilled the orange juice. She would only have been shocked if it was fact and she had hoped it would never come to light.'

'Things do not come to light, light comes to them. You believe she spoke to and met Kerr before his death?'

'It wouldn't have been afterwards.'

'The repetition of an inane remark.'

'But the way you asked . . .'

'Did you accuse her of murdering Kerr?'

'Had I done so, she would have become exceedingly upset.'

'When a person is distraught, she is most likely inadvertently to speak the truth.'

'That's not a sympathetic attitude.'

'You believe sympathy is good reason for being diverted from your duty?'

'It's not so long since you wrote that all officers must show compassion to those they question.'

'Compassion is not another word for incompetence. Am I correct to believe the only certain result of your questioning the señora is that she spilt orange juice over her no doubt very expensive dress?'

'Because it showed she was shocked . . .'

'Your supposition. An alternative would be that she heard far too much about the local history, for which few can have any interest, but you lacked the social savoir faire to realize this; she spilled the juice in order to provide an excuse to ask you to leave.'

'Rather an excessive method of persuading me to do so, señor.'

'A measure of her distress. You will return and resume your questioning of her. Should she spill more orange juice over herself, you will stay until she has changed and then continue your questioning.'

SIXTEEN

On Tuesday, there was a cold wind from the north, light drizzle, and snow on Puig Major. Alvarez sat at his desk and wondered how he would spend the millions he would win on the next lottery draw. Dolores could employ a woman to do all the housework and menial jobs which were part of cooking while she devoted herself to producing ever greater dishes. Jaime could officially retire instead of unofficially. Juan and Isabel would, as adults, be financially supported. He could give up work. Buy a farm. Hire men to do the physical work while he watched the sowing, the harvesting . . .

The telephone rang. He left the hectares of rich land, returned to the small office, lifted the receiver. 'Inspector Alvarez, Cuerpo General de Policía.'

'Appleby, Interpol officer. Do you speak English?'

'Fairly well, I hope.'

'Then it's likely better than half the English do. You asked for enquiries to be made concerning Colin Kerr and provided details of his passport and entry date into Spain. The British police were able to identify him. I'll email his full criminal CV, but in brief, he started his criminal career when young; grew ambitious; was caught trying to rob a supermarket and suffered a ridiculously short sentence, yet it still changed his lifestyle. He was described as good looking, had a very agile tongue, and women were attracted to him. He started on the until-death-do-us-part routine. He found a woman with some money, often newly widowed and depressed, wormed his way into her affections, married her, grabbed all her money and departed. It's thought he married and defrauded at least five women.

'One of the victims complained to the police, and they were interested in him when the father of a previous "wife" met him in a pub, rammed a broken bottle into his neck. He spent

several weeks in hospital, and on leaving was charged with
perjury, theft and bigamy – his final bigamous marriage being
with a nurse, Laura Dorothy Lomas, who had looked after
him in hospital and was credited with having saved his life
when he suffered a sudden tear in an artery. Not a man to
show gratitude! The magistrates at the preliminary hearing,
for a reason no one could understand, granted him bail. He
naturally disappeared.'

A silence.

'Are you still there?'

'I'm sorry, señor, but what you have told me is . . . very
disturbing.'

'It's a wrong identification?'

'On the contrary, I am certain it is a correct one.' He thanked
Appleby.

What significance was there in a name? Had she not known
Kerr, would he judge there to be any? Yet how to ignore the
fact that Laura Lomas had been a nurse, as had Laura Ashton?

Like Benavides, he wished he had not done what he had.

The phone rang. His mind so occupied in self-inspired
despair, it was if he was acting involuntarily when he lifted
the receiver. He said nothing.

'Alvarez?' Salas demanded.

He did not answer.

'Who is on the line?'

Reaching through despair, he mumbled his name.

'Are you drunk?'

'I wish I was.'

'Alvarez –' Salas' tone had changed from annoyance to an
emotion approaching concern – 'are you ill?'

'No, señor.'

His tone returned to normal. 'Do you accept you have
knowingly and deliberately disobeyed my orders?'

'In what respect?'

'You need to determine to which occasion I am referring?
I have just been informed that you requested Interpol to provide
information concerning Kerr. Is that correct?'

'Yes.'

'Did I not say that was unnecessary?'

'You were wrong, señor.'

'A junior officer does not tell his superior chief that he is wrong.'

'If you don't believe you were—'

'Can you explain your inexcusable disobedience?'

'I don't think it was.'

'I ordered you not to get in touch with Interpol.'

'You didn't specifically forbid me from contacting them, señor, and I considered it essential to learn if there was anything about Kerr's life that was relevant to this case.'

'You should not be surprised to learn that I am considering whether it would be in the best interests of the Cuerpo to treat your disobedience with just severity.'

'All I've—'

'You are unwilling to appreciate it is insolent to contradict your senior's judgement, believing it to be of less value than your own?'

'But as I've learned—'

'I will take time to determine my future course of action in regard to your behaviour.'

'Señor . . .'

'I have nothing more to say.'

'It appears possible that Kerr had been married to Señora Ashton.'

There was a silence.

'How do you know that?' Salas finally demanded.

'Interpol are providing a CV of Kerr, but they gave me a résumé on the phone. Kerr was a small-time crook who was jailed. When he came out, he changed course and set about finding women who were single or newly widowed and had money, used his agile tongue to persuade them to marry him. After defrauding each one of all she had, he left in search of another victim.

'The father of one met him by chance, jammed a broken bottle into his neck. He went to hospital where his life was saved by a nurse whom he soon married. Laura Dorothy Lomas.'

'When was this?'

'Approximately three years ago.'

'Have you understood the full significance of what we have learned?'

'We, señor?'

'The course of events can now provisionally be plotted. Laura Lomas, defrauded and abandoned by Kerr, bigamously married Señor Ashton because of his wealth. They came to live on the island, perhaps at her instigation since it would be safer for her than remaining in England. Kerr, when out of jail, managed to learn where she now was, married to money. He came to the island, demanded she pay him for his silence or he would inform her husband that he was not legally married to her. Since his will bequeathed by far the largest part of his estate to his beloved wife, without naming her, she could not inherit since she was not his wife. She paid the first blackmail demand, getting the money from her husband with lies since she was too scared to explain the situation. Further demands from Kerr were bound to follow. Her husband was ill and could not be expected to live very much longer. Should her true status become known before he died – she lacked the honesty to tell him the truth – he might very well change his will and she would inherit nothing. If it became known shortly after his death, the law would hold she was not entitled to inherit under the terms of the will. Kerr had to die. She found a way of persuading him to ingest prussic acid when out with her in the yacht, dropped his body over the side.'

'It could seem that was what happened, but it has to be wrong.'

'Why?'

'She could never kill for any reason.'

'A woman's mind will find good reason to do anything.'

'Her character . . .'

'There is no need to repeat what you have said many times. However, I will repeat what *I* have said. Guilt is judged by facts, not emotional judgements.'

'In her case . . .'

'Alvarez, are you betraying your duty by allowing regrettable desire to deny fact?'

'I'm not certain what you mean.'

'Are you emotionally interested in Señora Ashton?'

'When she is so newly widowed; so distressed? I admire her, that's all.'

'And the chance to enjoy her wealth?'

'If that were so, I should not have tried to find out more about Kerr. Your comment is completely unjustified, señor.'

'I decide what is justified. Have you asked the señora to explain why she has never identified Kerr as her true husband?'

'No. As yet, there is no certainty that he was her husband. The two Christian names are similar; but individually they must be common, and together not uncommon but very unlikely to be unique. Both were nurses, but how many thousands of nurses will there be in Britain?'

'That is reason not to question her?'

'I think there has to be more evidence before I challenge her on so emotional a level.'

'Her emotions are of no account.'

'I'll bet my life she could not murder anyone.'

'A wager of minimum value. My friend, the learned psychologist, said when last we discussed the errant mind, and your name was mentioned, that an imagination which is blind to reality often denotes either a gambling or a criminal tendency. Do you gamble?'

'Very seldom as I am a born loser. Yet, stupidly, I did buy a ticket in the Cuerpo lottery.'

'What is that?'

'A draw for the name of the next comisario.'

'On such a subject, a regrettable and demeaning lottery.'

'Very regrettable for me, señor. I did succeed in drawing a name, but he's as likely to gain further promotion as a duck is to crow.'

'What name did you draw?'

'I would rather not say.'

'Your judgement of any superior chief is, of course, of no consequence. However, there is one man who should never be considered for promotion since he owed his present rank to influence, not talent. Perhaps you drew Superior Chief M?'

'No, señor.'

'To suffer a severe rebuke, when fully justified, and the inability to command with the necessary respect for others,

provide a considerable disadvantage. It is very likely it was
Superior Chief T's name you drew?'

'No.'

'Then . . . you are wasting your time, which is of little
account, and my time, which is of much account.' Salas
accepted the remaining names had become too few for him
to risk continuing. 'Detail your intended movements in the
investigation into the Kerr case.'

'At the moment, things are so confused it's difficult to know
which way to turn.'

'Standing still will not be an option. You will address the
señora again, this time as the prime suspect. You will question
her strongly, assiduously, without thought of emotional distress
and without reliance on assumption or supposition.'

'I just don't believe she can be the prime suspect.'

'Your belief is immaterial. Clearly, either you have failed
to understand the significance of the information we have
received, or you are trying to ignore it. Kerr blackmailed her
once. It was obvious he would continue to blackmail her until
she had nothing left with which to buy his silence. He had to
die, and quickly, if her comfortable life was not to turn into
hardship.'

'One cannot ignore the other suspects.'

'If one is prepared to accept your reports, there is none.'

'Each of the servants benefited from the señor's death.
Browyer was, and is, deeply resentful . . .'

'I need to remind you, once again, that you are investigating
Kerr's murder, not Señor Ashton's natural death?'

'Señor, I have explained why the smaller bequests in the
señor's will might be connected with Kerr's murder.'

'And you have assured me that they were not.'

'I could have been wrong.'

'A probability, not a possibility.'

'If I have a word with each member of the staff . . .'

'You will question Señora Ashton and make it clear that
she is suspected.'

SEVENTEEN

Jaime emptied his glass, noticed Dolores might be about to enter the room, did not pick up the bottle of Ferrer and refill it. 'Did you read how well we did against Llubi?' he asked.

Alvarez did not answer.

Jaime repeated the question.

'At what? Knocking down coconuts?'

'Have you lost your marbles? At football.'

She came in and put cutlery and plates on the table.

'Enrique's a thousand kilometres away,' Jaime said. 'Dreaming of the forty sweet young virgins awaiting him.'

'How right my mother was when she said that after the third drink, silence is to be preferred, but seldom granted.'

'I've only had one.'

'How right she was.' She returned into the kitchen.

Jaime refilled his glass. He leaned across the table and snapped his fingers.

Alvarez started.

'We've been sitting here for a quarter of an hour and you haven't said a word.'

'I'm hellish worried.'

'You've got a woman looking anxiously at the calendar? Or is it that one in Son Dragó again? You can't persuade her she's the attraction, not her money?'

There was a call from the kitchen. 'My grandmother used to say—'

Jaime interrupted. 'Your grandmother?'

'That is what I said.'

He lowered his voice. 'Why bother with the grandmother when the mother is on every channel, all the time?'

'What was that?' Dolores called.

'I was wondering what she might have said.'

'That a man's mind concentrates on one subject.'

'Why not, when it's so interesting?'

'My grandmother would not have been surprised by your remark.'

Jaime drank. He spoke quietly to Alvarez. 'DNA has made it difficult for a man to wriggle out of things, but there are still one or two ways.'

'It's work that's blacking my life, not women.'

'Then your priorities are haywire.'

'The superior chief is so certain she's guilty, but she can't be. She's too genuine, straight, honest, and cares too much for others.'

'I suppose you mean the Son Dragó woman? She doesn't sound normal from what you've just said.' Jaime thought for a moment. 'Didn't you say she had been a nurse? She ought to be able to give you some tips—'

'On what?' Dolores asked as she stepped through the bead curtain.

'On persuading Salas he's hopelessly wrong,' Alvarez said hastily, to prevent Jaime from attempting to answer.

'Have you not told him so?' she asked.

'He seldom listens to anything I say.'

'Then he is even more stupid than it seems. You are a man to be listened to. Supper will be very soon so there is no need to drink any more.' She returned into the kitchen, leaving the strands of the bead curtain knocking into each other with diminishing frequency.

A compliment from Dolores was rare and to be savoured. But it offered no defence against the coming interview.

He drove very slowly along Roca Nesca. The sun was shining, the bay was deep blue, the mountains friendly in appearance, and the wake of power boats and the sails of yachts and sailboards provided a cocktail of colour. The setting for a man who sought perfection, but a bitter contradiction for the man who dreaded the immediate future.

Benavides met him at the front doorway. 'If you want to speak to the señora, she left.'

Had she realized disaster was close behind and fled to try

to escape it, proving how wrong he had been in his judgements? 'Have you a forwarding address?'

'You misunderstand me, inspector. She was in great need of a break, having been greatly disturbed since your last visit. Since I blame myself, I discreetly suggested she went somewhere where she would not constantly be reminded of all that has happened.'

'You know where she has gone?'

'To stay with friends.'

'You have their name and address?'

'She did not think it necessary to tell me who they were or where they live.'

'How long will she be away?'

'Almost certainly not for as many days as she should be.'

Alvarez's relief at not yet having to name her a murderess might be cowardly, but was great. 'Since I'm here, I'll have another word with you and the others.'

'With respect, I am certain we have told you all we can.'

'That doesn't stop me having to ask.'

They went through the hall and into the staff sitting-room. As Alvarez sat, he said: 'I want to go over all you have previously told me.'

'May I ask why?'

'In the hope of learning something, perhaps so minor that only now can I understand its significance, which will name someone with a stronger motive for murdering Kerr than the señora.'

Benavides spoke angrily. 'You can believe she is any way guilty of Kerr's death?'

'I am convinced she had no part in it. But innocence has to be based on fact, not emotion.'

'Is it what you learned from me which makes you question her innocence?'

'That is only in part responsible. Fresh evidence has turned up.'

'What evidence?'

'I will only say it makes the señora's involvement in the death of Kerr appear more likely to some.'

'Who?'

'Those whose minds are closed by certainty. I have to prove them wrong, which is why I need to question you, and the others, further.'

'Very well. I will do anything and everything possible to help you.'

'Why?'

'I do not understand.'

'Why would you willingly incriminate someone?'

'That is not obvious? I would as soon see Beatriz blamed for the sad, but natural death of the señor, for whom she, and the rest of us, had such respect, as for the señora to be thought guilty of Kerr's murder.'

'Have you any reason to modify what you told me about knowing nothing with regard to the contents of the señor's will?'

'No.'

'Were you incorrect when you denied ever having considered that the señor, being so generous a man, might leave you something by way of thanks for your years of service?'

'Inspector, when there was so much suspicion, I was misled into thinking that the least said, the better.'

'You had wondered?'

'I fear so.'

'Were you in debt when Kerr died?'

'I have a savings account in which are already several thousand euros. Do you wish to know the account and its number in order to confirm I am not lying?'

'I believe you.'

'Occasionally?'

Alvarez smiled. 'We are expected to disbelieve. Did you in fact know where the señor kept the keys of the safe?'

'"Occasionally" was the wrong word,' Benavides said bitterly. 'It should have been "never". Do you once again wonder if I bribed Kerr to break into the safe and then murdered him to keep him quiet? The idea is so goddamn stupid that only a—' He stopped abruptly, paused, said calmly: 'I apologize, inspector.'

'It's nothing.'

'I was disturbed that you could imagine . . . believe I could . . .'

'As my boss would say, imagination seldom shakes hands with facts. I need to have another word with the others. Is Inés here?'

'I'm not certain.'

'Are you trying to shield her again?'

'García has the mind of a peasant.'

'Those of us from the island mostly do, but what has his mind to do with Inés?'

'He learned why you knew Kerr had been to the house and stupidly told Inés what a fool she was, in language which exacerbated her feeling of guilt. She has not yet come back to work.'

'Has anyone found out how she is?'

'Beatriz went to where she lives. Inés was so disturbed, Beatriz spent a long time with her, and as a result, lunch was not ready when it should have been. I explained and apologized to the señora on Beatriz's behalf.'

'How did the señora respond?'

'As one would expect. A doctor was to visit Inés at once and she was not to restart work until she felt fully able to do so.'

'It's good to know. I'll have a word with Beatriz now.'

'She is preparing lunch.'

'Far more important than speaking to me! What's the meal today?'

'I cannot say.'

'I expect it will be excellent. I do not need to speak to María or Raquel again right now, so that leaves García. I didn't notice him when I arrived. Is he here today?'

'Yes. Perhaps he was having his *merienda* in his garden shed when you drove up.'

'I'll find out.'

After a seven minutes' walk Alvarez came within sight of the large garden hut. As he approached, García stepped out of it and roughly asked: 'You want something?'

'Sorry to interrupt your *merienda*, but whilst you're finishing it, we can have a chat.'

'Better things to do.'

'You'd rather we had it at the post?'

'You think talk like that scares me?'

'You're not bothered about your own best interests?'

García reluctantly returned into the hut, sat. 'There's nothing to drink.'

'I wouldn't expect there to be,' Alvarez answered as he settled on the cane chair. 'Do you remember telling me you hadn't ever seen Kerr, didn't know he'd been to Son Dragó?'

'What of it?'

'If that were true, why berate Inés in peasant language for telling me about Kerr's visit?'

García leaned over to a battered basket and brought out an unopened bottle of wine.

'Nothing to drink? A man who tries not to offer a *copa* of wine to a visitor has to come from Mestara.'

'I told you I was born in Estart.'

'Almost as good an explanation.'

'You reckon you're smart?'

'If I did, the weight of opinion would correct me.'

García brought a corkscrew and one glass from the basket. 'No good offering you any since it ain't from Rioja but made at home.'

'I choose home brew every time; it tastes of earth, which is the island's gold.'

'You ought to be in a nuthouse, not the Cuerpo.'

'Some say it's difficult to differentiate the two institutions.'

'You want some wine?'

'I'll not refuse the kind offer.'

García filled the glass, handed it to Alvarez. 'Hope the earth bloody well chokes you.' He brought a second glass out of the basket.

They drank.

Alvarez was the first to speak. 'You told me that when there were ripe nuts on the bitter almond trees, there was always a notice warning people not to break 'em and eat the almonds.'

García said nothing.

'Did you never forget to set up the notice; never once wake up thick-headed after a prolonged *merienda* in this hut and wonder if you had remembered it?'

'It's easy to see how you work.'

'I'm asking how *you* do since I've been told that the notice wasn't always there. Was my informant lying? If so, I'll have heavy words with him.'

García drained his glass. 'Maybe I ain't saying there couldn't have been a time when I wasn't up to it, being sick.'

'Navigating the negatives, you accept there have been times when the notice has not been on show because of too much wine?'

'Once. On account of flu.' He refilled his glass.

Alvarez waited for his to be refilled, finally accepted it would not be. 'You burned the nuts you knocked down from the bitter almond trees?'

He drank.

'Likely you could have forgotten to do that after a night out?'

'I don't do nights out.'

'Then you're married. It's strange how wives don't like husbands to have a little fun in a bar.'

'So I never forgot to burn 'em, as you're trying to say.'

'You've never even left them overnight, to be cleared the next morning?'

'No.'

'Did the señor ever talk to you about them?'

'It was him made me put up the notice every day and burn the nuts I knocked down. Being a foreigner, he didn't understand us islanders aren't so bloody daft as to eat them.'

'Some people gain pleasure from flirting with danger.'

'You're talking stupid.'

'Do you smoke?'

'What of it?'

'Smoking and drinking are flirting with danger.' Alvarez brought out from his pocket a pack of cigarettes, offered it.

García withdrew a cigarette. 'It's what the lads are bringing into the coves now, then?'

'This pack has a government seal.'

'So does vodka at five euros a bottle. Only it wasn't the government slapped on the seal.'

'Who's selling it at that price?'

'Can't say.'

'Withholding information concerning a criminal offence is a serious crime.'

'Can't tell what I don't know.'

Since Alvarez did not like vodka, he saw no point in pursuing the subject. 'Was the señora interested?'

'What in?'

'The bitter almonds.'

'Once wanted to know how many was fatal. That's all.'

'What did you answer?'

'Said no one what's learned has ever been back to tell.'

'Strange she should have asked you.'

'Strange only to someone what thinks crookedly.'

'Doesn't seem a question one would normally ask.'

'You know what's normal, when people come here on an open day and try to find a few bitter almonds because they want to know what they taste like?'

'Has anyone else ever asked you the same question as the señora did?'

'Bloody near everyone who sees me. I tell 'em, eat one and you'll see double, eat two and you won't see anything.'

'You're grossly overrating the potency of a nut.'

'You ain't got the mind to reckon I maybe say wrong because it'll stop 'em trying a nibble or two and learning what guts' ache is?'

'If you knew who poisoned Kerr, would you tell me the name?'

'Wouldn't bother if it didn't bother me.'

'Francisco Matias wrote, "Because man leans to injustice, democracy and truth are needed to straighten him."'

'All democracy does is allow us to kick out one bunch of thieves and let in another.'

'You seem to have an unfortunate outlook on life.'

'Sitting here with you don't offer me anything else.'

Whatever García claimed, Alvarez decided, he must have been born in Mestara.

EIGHTEEN

Alvarez rang at a reasonable time in the morning.
'Señora Ashton's residence,' Benavides pompously announced.
'Inspector Alvarez. Has the señora returned?'
'Not yet.'
Alvarez experienced a cowardly relief. 'I'll be over later to have a word with Beatriz. Will María or Raquel be with you today? I do have to speak to them again'
'Raquel will be here.'
'Ask her not to go before I have a word with her.'
'Very well, inspector.'
He phoned Hotel Floris. 'Is Señor Browyer still a guest?'
'One moment, please.'
He tried to judge how long it could be before making a further report to Salas.
'Señor Browyer is leaving after lunch to return to England.'
'Ask him to remain at the hotel until I get there. I wish to speak to him.'
'Very well.'
'I'll be with you in an hour.' The drive would take half an hour, but *merienda* should never be hurried.

Browyer was pacing the hotel foyer. When Alvarez greeted him, his reply was a nervous, weak twitch of the mouth and a nod.
'I won't keep you for long so there's no worry you'll miss your lunch.' Had it been he, lunch would have been a doubtful option.
'You're not . . . not . . .'
'Arresting you? I think not.'
Browyer used a handkerchief to clear sweat from his forehead.
'Your room will be empty until later on, when the next load of tourists are due, so we'll go on up to it. Four one four?'

'I . . . I can't remember.'

The room had not yet been prepared. A battered suitcase and holdall were on the floor by the unmade bed. Alvarez sat on that. Browyer remained standing. 'I don't understand . . .'

'Last time we spoke, I learned you frequently came to the island and stayed with your uncle in the hopes of persuading him to give you more money in the guise of borrowing it; also, probably, hoping to persuade him to change his will in some degree to your favour.'

'That's not fair.'

'Why not?'

'I never mentioned his will to him.'

'You expect me to believe that?'

'I . . . Well, I didn't say anything so direct.'

'A man for circumspection. Is there anything else you told me that needs a little clarification?'

'I never saw him smoke anything.'

'Which was correct.'

'What more do you want? I can't tell you what I don't know.'

'I will accept that. Tell me what kinds of almond trees grow in the grounds at Son Dragó.'

'Kinds?'

'Yes.'

'They were all the same except for two or three.'

'What was different about them?'

'They were supposed to bear poisonous nuts.'

'Who told you that?'

'There was a notice to that effect. It was a bit scary. I couldn't understand why the trees were allowed to grow.'

'Did you ever see the gardener knocking down the almonds from them with a long bamboo pole?'

'I might have done.'

'You can't be certain?'

'I did talk to him but he became so rude . . . I remember it was when he was knocking them down that he picked up a handful from the ground and asked me if I'd like to eat several and find out if they really were dangerous. I told my uncle the gardener had tried to kill me and he should be sacked. My uncle just laughed, said Mallorquins had a queer sense of humour and the few nuts in his hand could do little more than remind me I was mortal.'

'Thank you. You've told me all I need to know. I hope your luncheon here will be an enjoyable one.'

'They're serving paella for those of us who are leaving. I hope I can have something else.'

'You don't like paella?'

'The thought of eating snails makes me feel sick.'

'One made with snails will be too expensive a dish to be served here. You'll find it contains rice, fish or chicken, onions, garlic, peas, peppers, perhaps something more, but not the sniff of a snail.'

'I'll be glad to get back home and have a decent meal.'

Raquel Valles entered the staff sitting-room. 'Manuel says you want to talk to me again?'

'Thanks for coming along.'

She sat, carefully hitching down her short skirt.

Unnecessary, he thought, but like most women, she flattered herself by believing a man always looked at her with exploring eyes. 'I'd like to know whether the señora ever showed much interest in the garden?'

'I'd say she likes it as much as the señor did. She often tells me when something is flowering, asks have I seen it, if not, I'm to go and look at it.'

'You quite often walk in the garden, then?'

'As often as possible. Sometimes, when my work's over, I spend maybe as much as an hour there. It seems to be full of peace: start off worried by this and that, and before long there aren't any problems. You won't understand, like as not.'

'On the contrary. I'm a countryman and know that, when everything seems to have gone wrong, sitting in a field and watching a flock of sheep and lambs can do a power of good for the soul. On your walks, do you usually go to the end of Roca Nesca?'

'When there's time.'

'Past the bitter almond trees?'

'Yes.'

'Have you ever noticed that the warning notice about the
almonds was missing?'

'No.'

'You'll have seen Felipe knocking them down?'

'Once or twice.'

'Does he collect them up and remove them?'

'Ask him.'

'You've not seen him do so?'

'Yes.'

'Have you ever noticed them lying about the place?'

'Felipe collects them up and burns them. He'd have to be
dead behind the forehead to leave them lying around.'

'Have you ever tried a bitter almond to see what it tastes
like?'

'When a friend of my grandmother was starving during the
war and ate so many she died?'

Sunshine came through the open window in a wide beam
and began to reach where she sat. It highlighted the soft curve
of her breasts under the light summer maid's uniform. The
first coupe in which to serve champagne had reputedly been
modelled on Marie-Antoinette's breast. If one wished to
modernize . . .

'Something interesting you?' she asked sharply.

'I was thinking.'

'Obviously.'

'About glasses.'

'Magnifying ones?'

'I don't think there's anything more I need ask you.'

'Satisfied you're wasting your time?'

She would never understand he had been appreciating
nature's art, not lusting.

He drove to Ca'n Llop, walked up the chipped-stone path to
the enlarged caseta, a building of strength, but no grace. A
ratter – a local breed of island dog – ran out and briefly barked
at him. He spoke to it, bent down and offered his hand; after
some hesitation, he was allowed to stroke it. Unfortunately,
Dolores was so house-proud, no dog would ever be welcomed.

María Patera stepped through the doorway.

'You'll remember me,' he said.

She nodded, looked down at the dog. 'Pedro's seldom friendly with a stranger. Even though you are a policeman, perhaps you are a good man.'

'A very difficult combination.'

She smiled; the smile by which he remembered her. 'You will come in and have a drink?'

'I was hoping to be given the chance.'

During the course of drinking two tumblers of wine, they discussed the government, the rise in prices of everything, the growing amount of land abandoned to weeds – a sight which would have horrified their parents – and the recent accusation of bribery made against the mayor of a nearby village.

The ratter jumped on to his lap.

'He never does that!' she exclaimed.

He was proud to be chosen, fondled the dog's ears. 'You told me you worked part-time at Son Dragó.'

'Me and Raquel each do three days.'

'You clean the rooms and sometimes help Beatriz in the kitchen?'

'I'm not going to say I like dusting, sweeping, cleaning, but I'd rather do that than be in the kitchen when something goes wrong with the cooking.'

'Manuel says she can be rather fierce.'

'I've heard her swear stronger than any man.'

'When you tidy a room, I suppose you often open cupboards to put something in, like a clean dress?'

'Cupboards, but not drawers. If there's something to put away in them, the señora prefers to do it herself.'

'Have you ever come across a collection of almonds in a cupboard?'

'In a bedroom? They're kept in the storeroom.'

'And if they're bitter almonds?'

'Straight into a bonfire, that's where they go, after Felipe's knocked them down.'

'You've never seen any in the señora's bedroom?'

'And I ain't seen a Christmas cactus either. You ask some daft questions for a man who likes a good home-made wine.'

'I have to.'

'Why?'

'Somebody poisoned Kerr and I need to find out who.'

'And you think . . .? Them questions about bitter almonds in her bedroom . . . Don't you understand it's more likely to have been me than her, and I didn't even know he existed until he was found dead?'

'Then you'd no reason to know Kerr scared her?'

'Why should I have done?'

'When very disturbed, she might have said something which made you realize he frightened her.'

'She never mentioned him.'

'It's possible that—'

'Seems anything's possible for you. Maybe you think Santa Ana wielded a flaming sword to sweep the Moors out of the village and it wasn't the people who did that?'

'Perhaps she was helping. Did the señora talk about her life in England?'

'Sometimes.'

'What did she say about it?'

'Mostly that she was a hundred times happier here.'

'Nothing more?'

'Only what it was like nursing people when some was grateful, others cursed and even tried to attack her. Has to be a strange country when there's people like that.'

'No mention of boyfriends?'

'When she was married to the señor? It ain't surprising Raquel says as you . . .' She stopped abruptly.

'Yes?'

'Can't remember what she said.'

'Try harder.'

'I ain't going to say when I don't know if you'd be pleased or angry.'

He failed to work out what could raise such opposing possibilities.

The weather changed rapidly. By the early evening, the sky was clear, the sun was shining warmly, tables, chairs, and overhead sunshades were set in front of Café Tomás on the northern side of the old square. He watched the tourists, vaguely but sufficiently irritated they should enjoy leisure while he had to work so hard, crossed to a vacant table and sat. Obviously not a foreigner, he was ignored until he called a waiter over. For some reason, too incredible to explain, he ordered a chocolate sundae instead of a brandy.

He wondered if he had moved into a parallel universe.

The waiter returned, put the shaped glass filled with ice cream, cream and chocolate sauce topped with a wafer on the table, spiked the bill. Alvarez stared at the sundae. If he could not order a coñac in a parallel world, of what other necessities might he be deprived? He called the waiter back. 'A coñac with just ice.'

'Why didn't you ask for that the first time and save me trouble?'

The waiter did not quickly reappear. Shoving the shover, as the old saying put it; expressing his annoyance at having to make an extra unnecessary trip into the café. When he brought the brandy, he spiked the bill with such force that the table juddered.

Alvarez drank, satisfied and grateful he was not in a parallel universe. Ordering an ice cream had been due to one of those blips in the mind to which anyone could be subject.

Inés, with a young woman of her own age, walked down the sloping road at the side of the raised square; she was laughing and looked happy. When she saw him, the laughter stopped.

'Hullo,' he said.

She muttered an inaudible reply.

'Would you both like to come on up and have an ice cream?'

She shook her head. Her friend said something in a low tone, put her arm around Inés and almost frogmarched her to the head of the square and then along to his table. They sat. Matilde was a chatterbox. Inés had told her he was a detective, she said. Was that true? Was it exciting?

He called the waiter and asked them what they would like. Matilde chose a chocolate sundae similar to the one he had, which was wilting badly despite being in the shade of the umbrella. Inés, unable to decide, finally agreed to have the same. He said he would have another brandy. As the waiter left, he suggested they shared his ice cream which, as they could see, he had not started. Matilde immediately accepted the offer; Inés did not share it.

As he watched them walk away, twenty minutes later, he wondered if Inés would gain self-confidence as she grew older. He doubted it. Or that her father would ever accept he was to blame.

He finished his second brandy, pulled the bills off the spike, mentally added up the totals and wondered how he could have been such a fool as to eat and drink at a tourist café.

He rang Palma.

'Superior Chief Salas is not in his office,' Ángela Torres announced.

'I'll speak to him tomorrow morning.'

'You may make a preliminary report to me.'

'I have been very busy questioning people . . .'

'Name those you have questioned.'

He was convinced she thought he would only be able to give one name. 'Benavides, who is the butler at Son Dragó—'

'You do not need to identify the position of the person concerned. I am aware what that is.'

'García, Patera, Valles. And Beatriz,' he added, to make up numbers.

'You did not question Señora Ashton?'

'She is away, staying with friends to have a break from all her problems and sorrow.'

'You have not spoken to her over the phone?'

'She did not tell anyone where she was going or who she was staying with.'

'That seems very unlikely.'

'If you need to corroborate the facts, perhaps you'll phone Benavides, who you will know is the butler.'

'The superior chief expects his juniors to carry out their own tasks, not rely on others to do them.'

'All I was—' He did not have the chance to explain. She had replaced the receiver.

The children were late back for supper. Dolores reproved them; it was rude to keep others waiting. She served *Salsa verda para pescado*. The fish was tuna, the sauce parsley, garlic, paprika, lemon juice, olive oil and salt.

'I've had a busy day,' Alvarez said.

Isabel giggled.

'There's no need for that,' Dolores said quietly.

Juan giggled.

'And the same applies to you.' Her tone had become sharper. They looked down at their plates. 'Very busy,' Isabel murmured. Juan tried not to giggle, ended up snorting.

'You will behave yourself or go into the kitchen to eat.'

Isabel said: 'We saw uncle earlier this evening.'

Juan sniggered.

Dolores hesitated between ordering them into the kitchen and learning why there should be amusement in their having seen Alvarez earlier.

'I didn't see either of you two,' Alvarez remarked.

They could not control their amusement and were sent into the kitchen with their plates.

'Were you wearing fancy dress?' Jaime asked.

Alvarez ignored Dolores' sharp look and refilled his glass.

'Why are the children behaving so stupidly?' she asked.

'I'm damned if I know.'

'And be damned if you don't,' Jaime added.

'Perhaps we should have a second kitchen,' she snapped, 'in order to accommodate the overflow from the first.'

'How d'you mean?'

'Of small moment. Tell the children they can come back in.'

'But they've only just gone out.'

'I should have remembered it is always quicker to do something myself than wait for you to decide to do as asked.' She went into the kitchen, returned with Juan and Isabel. The meal continued in near silence.

She collected up the plates and cutlery. 'Isabel, you can carry these through; Juan, take the breadboard and the barra. Thinking the family might like a treat, I bought some chocolate ice cream . . .' She stopped as the children once more sniggered.

She hit the table with the flat of her hand. 'Since no one will enjoy the treat while ill manners prevail, you two will explain what so rudely amuses you.'

They looked at each other.

'You do not wish to have any ice cream?'

Isabel spoke slowly, careful not to look at her brother. 'Two girls were having chocolate sundaes at Café Tomás.'

'If that is a cause for amusement, I fear we may suffer your stupidity until the end of the season.'

'Both of them,' Juan added.

'Many tourists eat and drink at that café.'

'They weren't much older than me and didn't look anything special.'

'To eat at a café for tourists for whom money is no object is very foolish but no cause for amusement.'

'Then uncle is very foolish?'

'Are you saying . . .? Isabel, you will help me with the ice cream.'

'Why can't Juan?'

Twenty minutes later, the table had been cleared except for two glasses, an ice bucket, and a bottle of Soberano, the children had gone out, and Dolores' expression was that of a rider who had just been told her horse was cow-hocked. Alvarez hastened to leave. 'I must get back to the post. With all the work—'

'You will leave when I have said what I have to say.'

'You won't want me.' Jaime began to stand, holding on to the edge of the table for balance. 'I promised to meet Tolo . . .'

'He will wait. Enrique, is it true you were in the square?'

'Yes, but—'

'You were at Café Tomás?'

'I suddenly felt I had to sit for a while.'

'Were there others at the table?'

'You're not going to start—'

'Was Juan correct to describe them as young girls?'

'If you think—'

'My thoughts are simple. For a man of your age to be in

the company of two young women who you are feeding chocolate sundaes, as a hunter uses bait, is contemptible; to do this
in full view of any passing villager is humiliating.'

'I gave them a good time in the hope they would give me
a good time? Is that what you think?'

'I do not wish to express my further thoughts.'

'You've just been doing so.'

'By tomorrow, everyone in the village will know about this
and our family will be shamed.'

'Would you care to listen to the facts before you get things
even more wrong?'

'I'll move and see if Tolo is still there,' Jaime said. He let
go of the table and took a pace towards the *entrada*.

'You will listen to what I have to say so that should you
be tempted by immoral thoughts to entertain a young lady – or
if, like Enrique, you know of no limit to licentiousness, *two*
young ladies – you will understand—'

Alvarez interrupted her. 'I was at Café Tomás when I saw
Inés with a friend. She is very naive and mentally overpowered
by her father who is some kind of cultist. She works at Son
Dragó because the señor and señora were kind enough to
employ her even though advised by the staff not to. I had not
met her friend, Matilde, before and will not be concerned if
I never meet her again. Conversation was carried on by her,
talking endlessly about nothing. And to make things quite
clear, I did not slip my hand under the table and—'

'You will not refer to such disgraceful action.'

'You accused me of shaming the family . . .!'

'I have no wish to continue the conversation.' She swept
out of the room.

'Now you've annoyed her so much, we'll likely be having
to eat garbanzos,' Jaime muttered.

'Do you never consider anything but your stomach? It
doesn't worry you two cents she got everything wrong when
she went for me?'

'Now she's away, let's hear what really happened. You
picked up one of 'em and the other tagged along and wouldn't
take the hint and clear off to leave you to get cracking?'

Alvarez poured himself another drink.

NINETEEN

T
he wind was strong, and the trees, shrubs and bushes along the drive to Son Dragó were in constant, irregular motion. The sea was equally restless; waves slapped Roca Nesca, sending spray sufficiently high that, at one point, Alvarez had to switch on the windscreen wipers.

He braked to a halt. He silently promised himself to forgo any drinks that day if Laura Ashton had decided to remain longer with her friends. As he left the car and walked to the front door, he added the further denial of cigarettes if Benavides informed him the señora would not be returning for several days and still could not name with whom or where she was staying.

Benavides opened the front door. 'Good morning, inspector. You wish to speak to Señora Ashton?'

'She has not returned?'

'She did so yesterday evening.'

What was the good of self-denial if there was no compensation? 'Perhaps her short break has not been as promising as she'd hoped?'

'If I may venture an opinion, she has returned in better spirits.'

'Yet you think it might be wise for me to wait a day or two before having another talk with her?'

'I should not like to give an opinion as to that, but in Valladolid we say "it will take twice as long tomorrow". Would you like to enter?'

He was shown into the sitting room. He looked through the nearer picture window and wished he was outside, in the fresh, salty wind.

Laura entered. 'Good morning, inspector.'

He returned the greeting. Her dress was in two dark, flat colours, which suited her as well as carrying the suggestion of mourning. She looked relaxed, spoke easily; when she sat,

she rested her arms on the chair. 'I hope things won't be as
dramatic as last time.'

'I . . . That is . . .'

His nervousness induced in her a sense of tension. She
began to fidget with the material of the chair arm. If it had to
be done, it was best done quickly. 'Señora, what was your
name before you married Señor Ashton?'

'How can that matter?'

'I should like to know.'

'For what reason?'

'I think that will become clear.'

Benavides entered. 'Would you wish for coffee, señora?'

'Yes, please. And the inspector might also like some.'

When Benavides briefly looked directly at him, Alvarez
'heard' the other's silent words. Treat her kindly; say nothing
to make her realize you can believe she might have murdered
Kerr.

Benavides left.

She said: 'If it's so important, I was christened Laura
Dorothy Lomas.'

'And when you married Señor Ashton, that was your name?'

'Why d'you think it could have been anything else?' she
asked sharply.

Had she not included 'Dorothy', he might have accepted
he had added coincidence to coincidence. 'It was not Laura
Dorothy Kerr?'

She made a mewling sound which came from the back of
her throat. 'No,' she denied shrilly.

'Señora, I have learned that Colin Kerr suffered a serious
injury to his neck and, in hospital, his life was saved by a
nurse. Were you that nurse?'

'No,' she answered. Her denial lacked all conviction.

'Did you marry Kerr?'

'You can't understand,' she said shrilly.

Benavides entered, offered the tray to Laura so she could
help herself to milk and sugar. He crossed to where Alvarez
sat, thrust the tray forward as he said: '*Picor de Satanás.*' He
left.

'Was he blackmailing you because Señor Ashton did not

know you were married when he met you in the hospital in which he was a patient? Señora, I should like to know.'

'No!'

He waited.

She stared at the carpet in front of her chair. 'Charles' wife died.'

He made no comment.

Her voice became calmer. 'Knowing that his mental pain would be worse than his physical pain, I gave him all the sympathy I could. When he left hospital, he insisted I went with him as a private nurse. One day, he . . . he proposed to me.

'I didn't know how to answer. I had come to like him very much – his strength of character, compassion, sense of humour – but his was a different world from the one I knew. I told him that people would say I was marrying him for his money. I still remember what he replied.'

'May I know what he said?'

'More damn fools if they're so small-minded they can't understand you're someone who could never sell herself.'

'You did not tell him you were married?'

'The houses in London, here, the Bahamas, the flat in New York; flying everywhere first class, staff to do the work, money to buy beautiful clothes . . . Perhaps I did sell myself.'

'No,' he said sharply. 'You would not have married him had you not been in love; luxuries would have counted for nothing.'

She looked up and at him. 'You believe that?'

'In the short time I have known you, señora, I have learned that you are totally honest.'

'When I didn't tell Charles before we were married? And I never regretted not having done so until . . .'

'Until, señora?'

'Manuel told me someone had phoned and wanted to speak to me, his name was Kerr. I was frightened and refused to answer that time. I desperately tried to believe the caller could not have been Colin. There had to be dozens of men with the surname Kerr. Then he turned up here. Manuel would not let him in. He came again, when Charles and Felipe were sailing. Colin said he needed money and if I'd give him five thousand euros, he'd forget we'd been married and had not divorced so my marriage to Charles was . . . was bigamous.'

'You paid the money?' he asked, knowing it had not been she.

'Charles gave me an allowance so I didn't have to ask for money every time I wanted to buy something, but I couldn't meet so large a demand. He was becoming very ill and I was terrified how he'd react if he learned we weren't legally married because he held old-fashioned moral values.'

'And since legally you were not his wife, you could not inherit under the unfortunate terms of his will.'

'You think that's what so desperately worried me? You believe it was money, not the hurt I'd cause him, which made me so desperate?'

'I spoke stupidly, señora. Even a second's thought would have prevented my suggesting such a possibility.'

'Charles became certain something was wrong with me, even though his mind had become vague. He asked me what it was. I tried to say I was just not feeling a hundred per cent, but he knew me too well to believe that. He said he knew he couldn't live much longer, and I must tell him what was the trouble so that he could try to put it right while he still had the time. I . . . I broke down and told him everything. Instead of hating me for not saying I was married when he proposed, instead of calling me a cheat, a liar who had been after his money, he made me sit down on the bed, took hold of my hands and said something which made me . . .

'He gave me the money. I handed it to Colin and asked him to leave the island and my life. He laughed. He wasn't going to get rid of a cow whilst it could still be milked. If I tried in any way to thwart his blackmailing, he'd make it public that I had never been Charles' legal wife and I'd be shut out of everything he owned.'

'He was wrong.'

'Don't you understand? The Spanish *abogardo* didn't realize that because of English law, he should have named me and not just referred to me as Charles' wife.'

'Señora, I asked the authorities in England to tell me what they could about Kerr's background. I learned he was a small-time crook. Good looking, presenting charm when he wanted to, he searched for a woman with some capital, recently bereaved or single and with few, if any, living relatives. He engaged her affections, married her, stole her money and disappeared. Only his marriage to the first victim was legal since she is known to still be alive. All later ceremonies were null and void. Your marriage to Señor Ashton was true since you were never legally married to Kerr.'

It was many seconds before she said: 'Oh, God! If only I'd known. Why only now?' Her body shook as she cried.

He left the room and its bitter sorrow, went out of the house and over to his car. As he started the engine, Benavides ran out of the house, banged on the door's window, and shouted: 'What have you been saying to her, you bastard?'

He drove away, his mind asking: what was it she had *not* said? That there would have been no need to kill Kerr?

Nurses knew full well the dramatic effect of poisons.

He poured out a large brandy and drank it before he dialled.

'Yes?' Ángela Torres said sharply.

'Inspector Alvarez. I need to speak to the superior chief.'

'Wait.'

Time elongated.

'Yes?' Salas demanded.

'Inspector Alvarez, señor. I have questioned members of the staff at Son Dragó and their evidence has not altered; they have confirmed all they have said before. The warning notice about the almonds was always in place. García knocked them down before there was any danger of their falling and immediately burned them.

'I have also questioned Señora Ashton. She had not informed Señor Ashton of her first marriage to Kerr until forced to do so by Kerr's blackmailing demands.'

'When was that?'

'Shortly before her husband died.'

'And Señor Ashton had not drawn up another will, naming her by her true surname so she could inherit his estate?'

'His mental condition had become confused and it's doubtful

it occurred to him to do this; in any case, a new will might not have been accepted because of that confusion.'

'You understand the significance of what you have just learned?'

'I think so.'

'I will assume the contrary. If Kerr died, she thought it unlikely that it would ever become known her marriage to Ashton was invalid and she should be able to inherit.'

'If she judged Kerr's death was the only solution, she would not have told her husband the truth.'

'Did she?'

'How d'you mean?'

'What proof is there that she did tell her husband?'

'One doesn't have proof of a private conversation unless it's taped.'

'Quite.'

'Why should she lie?'

'The answer escapes you?'

'Yes.'

'I am not surprised. Where there are staff, private conversations are potentially far from private. You will question them all as to whether one of them heard anything significant; perhaps one day the señor, whom you suggest had become less than mentally alert, did not guard his tongue sufficiently.'

'You still consider her a possible suspect?'

'The prime suspect. I would be at fault if I did not do so, as you are at fault in trying to deny the probability.'

'If you had met her, spoken to her, listened to her, you would understand she is incapable of such a crime.'

'I do not welcome my judgements being made by someone else. If she did not poison Kerr, who did? Name the possible suspects.'

'Benavides, García.'

'You know of no others?'

It occurred to him that he had forgotten to question Beatriz again. 'Inés, María, Raquel, Beatriz.'

'Why do you name men by their surnames, women by their Christian names?'

'It seems more respectful.'

'Respect is seldom remarked on this island. You have not mentioned Browyer. Have you decided to forget the absurd and irrational suggestion he murdered Kerr because he had been disinherited by the señor?'

'I am certain he lacked the intention or ability to poison Kerr.'

'You have named all potential heirs?'

'Llueso was left five thousand euros . . .'

'In an excess of wild imagination, you conceived the possibility one of the staff . . . I forget what was the supposition. I presume you no longer consider that, whatever it was?'

'I don't.'

'Then one must accept, as I have constantly reminded you, money must be the motive. Yet all those who had a hopeful interest in the estate are, in your judgement, innocent?'

'Yes.'

'Then either one of those whom you've named has fooled you or you have failed to identify a person who has a motive.'

'Señora Ashton did not kill Kerr.'

'And if I accept that?'

'You do agree I have been right from the beginning?'

'You did not hear me say the word "if"?'

'I am not sure what you are suggesting.'

'If you believe none of the suspects you have named is guilty, you have hardly carried out a competent investigation. You will start to do so by considering what I have tried to get you to understand: money will provide the motive.'

'Yet if everyone with any interest in the señor's estate is innocent . . .'

'You choose not to remember the little apophthegm I drew up as an invaluable aide-memoire for any detective of intelligence. When all that is impossible is eliminated, whatever remains has to be the truth, however improbable.'

'If you are using that to try to say the señora poisoned Kerr . . .'

'I am saying exactly that.'

'But if something is so improbable as to be impossible . . .'

'You have failed to understand the meaning of my neat apophthegm.'

'But—'

'There is no need to continue the conversation.'

Alvarez slowly replaced the receiver. What if he had understood it and Salas had not?

TWENTY

Alvarez poured himself another brandy, leaned back in the chair, put his feet up on the desk. Laura Ashton, far too disturbed in mind, had not understood the fear and hatred her confession brought her husband. Fear that after his death she would be financially ruined; hatred for the man who yielded the threat. He had given Laura the first payment of blackmail, decided to use the life left to him to make certain that was the last payment. Yet his physical condition had become so poor that when he had said he was going with García for a sail to enjoy one final moment on the water, no matter that it was dark, the staff had done everything they could to prevent his doing so.

Benavides stared at Alvarez with expressed anger. 'The señora is not at home.'

'I've come—'

'She has asked me to inform you that you are no longer welcome at Son Dragó.'

'I want a word with García, not her.'

'She would wish you to leave the estate immediately.'

'Is he here today?'

'I do not know.'

'I'll have a look around to find out if you missed his arrival.'

Benavides cleared his throat and spat.

Alvarez returned to his car, picked up a plastic bag in which was a bottle of Fundador, walked along Roca Nesca to the garden shed. It was empty, but nearby a man was swearing. By a century cactus, its central column marking its coming death, García held the broken shaft of a mattock.

'Getting violent?' Alvarez asked.

'Immature wood with the strength of bloody cardboard.'

'Nothing is as good as it used to be.'

'Not when you turn up every other minute.'

'It's *merienda* time.'

'I've a job to finish.'

'With a broken mattock?'

García looked at the plastic bag in Alvarez's hand. 'You wanting something?'

'A chat.'

'About what I've said a dozen times already?'

'Something more important.'

García ran the fingers of his left hand through his tangled, curly hair, picked up the mattock, walked to the garden shed, threw the pieces to the side of it, went inside.

Alvarez passed the bottle to García, who looked at the label and said disparagingly, 'You ain't flush with euros, then. What's the grub? Dry crusts of bread?'

'I haven't brought anything.'

'Then you won't be eating.' He lifted two glasses out of the cane basket, half filled one and passed it, poured a second drink for himself. 'What's got you messing up other people's working this time?'

'Your sailing experiences.'

'Ain't got none.'

'You went out with the señor in case of trouble from the engine.'

'Didn't happen often.'

'Tell me about your trip with the señor very shortly before he died.'

'Not been out in the boat for three, four weeks.'

'Where were you when he died?'

'At home.'

'Will your wife corroborate you?'

'You trying to drag her into it?'

'Merely pointing out that things can become tricky when one starts lying. Tell me about that night.'

'Just done.'

'I reckon it's a lie.'

'Reckon all you want.'

'Would you describe the señora as a good woman?'

'Don't come better, same as the señor.'

'It was she who said your daughter was to go to a clinica in Palma and paid the bills. Saved her life?'

'Likely.'

'A tragedy the señora should lose her husband and then fall into the present mess. One would have said she'd suffered enough. But life likes kicking someone who's down.'

'What are you on about?'

'She is the prime suspect for the death of Kerr. My superior is certain she poisoned him.'

'Then he ain't the brains to clean a *pozo negro*.'

'As he sees it, the evidence has to point to her being the murderess.'

'If you ain't got nothing but balls to tell, clear off.'

They drank. Alvarez held out his glass for a refill. García poured them both another drink. He brought a *barra* sandwich out of a plastic bag. 'Only got one.'

'There's still something in the bag.'

'What's going to stay in it.'

'There's more pleasure to be gained by giving than receiving.'

'You're the first copper I've heard talk about giving when he don't mean a ticket.'

'Perhaps the police in Estart aren't as kind as they are here.'

'With you around? What d'you want so as I can get on with work.'

'You haven't finished eating and I haven't started. You can pass over a bit of the *barra*.'

'Manuel says you're a real sod.' García tore off a section of the bread.

'That's because I offend his sense of dignity.'

'Because you're so goddamn stupid, you think the señora could have had anything to do with Kerr.'

'I am certain she had no part in his murder.'

'When Manuel said the señora was hysterical after you'd spoken to her?'

'Which is why I know she's innocent.'

'You have to kick a man before you ask him how he's feeling?'

'If I had not said what I did, I would not have learned she

has to be innocent. Manuel is judging me by his interpretation of the evidence. I'm here to contradict his interpretation.'

'Use a shotgun.'

'That would complicate matters. I'm hoping the truth which you will provide will succeed.'

'You think I know anything except she wouldn't ever go near Kerr?'

'Have you been doing a lot of cooking recently?'

'When I'm married?'

'There's a lot of ash and half burned wood outside.'

'What of it?'

'Been having barbecue parties?'

'You're talking shit.'

'Or maybe boiling up bitter almonds?'

'You want to see me in jail? You ain't going to.'

'I am trying to save the señora from being wrongly found guilty of murder. What was the fire for?'

García poured himself another drink.

'You don't owe her on account of your daughter?'

He called Alvarez a combination of names of such obscenity they were normally spoken only after knives had been drawn.

'Tell me the truth, Felipe, and give me the chance to save the señora.'

'And have you shout what I tell?'

'I will treat it as sacrosanct as is a confession to a priest.'

'You ain't no priest.'

'Would I be here if I were not doing everything possible or impossible to try to persuade that Madrileño he's wrong to suspect the señora?'

'D'you swear on your mother's grave that what I say will help the señora?'

'I swear I hope it will.'

After a couple of minutes, García drank, then said: 'Manuel told me the señor and señora had some sort of terrible trouble; she looked like she was desperate, he looked as if the pain was so fierce he couldn't die quickly enough. So when the señor, shortly before he did die, said he wanted me on the yacht because he was sailing, I said what all the others did, it was madness. But I went with him.

'There was a bottle of champagne in the tiny refrigerator and he opened it as we made for the Port. He offered me some. Said I didn't want any while we was afloat. He finished the bottle. Never before seen him drink like that. He said there was something had to be done and would I help him. He wasn't drunk, just not guarding his tongue. Said he'd be dead soon and he wasn't scared of that, but was terrified of what would happen to Laura. He called her Laura, straight out, not señora like usual.

'I didn't know whether to stop him talking if he wasn't sure what he was saying because of the booze . . . That's straight, inspector. I wasn't doing nothing to persuade him to tell more.'

'I believe you.'

García passed the bottle to Alvarez; there was only a token of brandy left in it. 'If he couldn't do something, Laura – called her that all the time – would be blackmailed until she hadn't a euro left, yet he had always hoped to leave her enough not to worry.'

'Did he explain why she was being blackmailed?'

'Muttered something.'

'A bigamous marriage?'

García drank. 'Seems there ain't much you don't know.'

'You haven't mentioned the bitter almonds.'

'Got a fag?'

Alvarez handed him a pack; he helped himself, struck a match for both of them.

'There wasn't no wind, and the señor stopped the engine in the middle of the bay. Said he had to do something to stop that bastard ruining the rest of Laura's life. He asked how dangerous was bitter almonds. Told him I didn't know how many one had to eat for 'em to be fatal, but it was a considerable number. He was quiet for a while then asked again if I'd help him. After what he and the señora had done for my daughter . . . He said to gather as many bitter almonds as there were.'

'Did he explain why?'

'No.'

'That was all he wanted?'

'Smash them into a mush; put that in water for a couple of

days, pressing hard down on it with weights. I was to go to the Peninsula and buy a distilling unit like students have.'

'Did you do as asked?'

'Yes.'

'You knew what you were doing?'

García shrugged his shoulders.

'What did you do with the distilled liquid?'

'Gave it to the señor. There wasn't much.'

'Did it have a smell?'

'Kind of.'

'What happened next?'

'I was to take him out in the yacht as soon as it started to get dark. The women said as that was ridiculous and he must stay in the house. He wouldn't listen. He was weak as a child, but he was still a man when he said what was to be done.'

'You sailed to where?'

'Tied up on the outside jetty of the marina. He told me to go to a letting agency and find out where Kerr was renting. I went there and found him smoking a reefer. Told him the señor wanted to discuss a financial settlement.'

'Did he hesitate?'

'No.'

'How would you describe him at that time?'

'In a hurry to get his hands on money.'

'The three of you set sail?'

'The señor gave me money for a taxi to my place.'

'You weren't worried about the señor sailing without you to help?'

'Didn't like him being without me if the wind suddenly got up and made things difficult, but he said what was to be.'

'To begin with, Kerr could have helped.'

'Didn't act like he knew which was the bows and which was the stern.'

'You watched the yacht leave, not knowing to where she was sailing?'

'Wasn't for me to know.'

'You thought the señor wanted to talk things over with Kerr and offer him money to forget blackmailing the señora any further?'

'Yes.'

Law and justice. Many said they were inextricably joined together. He lacked a lawyer's ability to defend that concept because life had taught him that the two could oppose each other.

The law demanded Ashton be named the murderer of Kerr. Justice said that Laura Ashton should not have to suffer the mental anguish of knowing what her husband had done in her defence.

As an inspector in the Cuerpo, he worked for the law, so his duty was clear. As Enrique Alvarez, he could not face the responsibility of not attempting to protect Laura from a lifetime of unjust guilt. 'Have you considered what would be her thoughts if she believed her husband had poisoned Kerr? He deserved to die, but that would not help her find the relief of justification. She would bear the guilt of understanding that if, years before, she had not made the mistake of giving way to sad loneliness and the guiles of Kerr, there would never have been reason to have to remember a loved husband as a murderer.'

'He was saving her from that sod,' García said forcefully.

'There's someone else in trouble if things go on as they are now.'

'Who?'

'When the señor asked you to turn the bitter almonds into a sodden mush and then distil the liquid, you knew why.'

'Didn't bother to think. Wasn't my business.'

'The law will say different.'

'You swore you wouldn't tell.'

'How can the señora be cleared of the pain of knowledge without detailing the evidence which proves she had none?'

'You bloody tricked me. You knew you was going to tell!'

'I am trying to work out how to save the señora without involving you.'

'You just said you can't.'

'If there were evidence that a stranger had been on the estate who'd wanted to know if Kerr was around, who clearly had some reason to hate Kerr, then in view of the lack of hard evidence against the señor – which only you can provide – then she could not remain a suspect.'

'There ain't been no one around asking.'

'You have said you haven't seen anyone, but when a man's as busy as you, has the worries of looking after the garden, making certain no one is at risk of eating a bitter almond, something which didn't seem important can slip the mind. And even if one might expect you later to remember an incident, why should you not decide it far too unimportant to tell me?'

'Who's going to take that?'

'Depends who's listening. If he's a senior officer, from Palma, or maybe Madrid, he'll believe Mallorquins are so stupid they can forget their own names. Still, supposing can't help the señora; only some kind of action can. Don't suppose you told anyone you were going to buy a distilling unit?'

'I ain't that stupid.'

'You paid in cash?'

'I said, the señor gave me euros.'

'Smash the unit and discard the bits in different waste bins.'

'But it's like it's just been bought, and it cost a lot.'

'Smash it, Felipe, and no one will come along and wonder why you need a distilling unit and try to find out what was in it. There's a load of wood ash outside. Scientists could be asked to examine it and find you'd been burning almond husks along with wood.'

There was a long pause.

'You ain't so stupid as you look,' García said.

'I hope to be able to return the compliment.'

TWENTY-ONE

Alvarez answered the phone.

'Is that you?' García asked.

'It is.'

'I saw a man—'

'Hang on. Who are you?'

'You bloody well know.'

'If you're making a report, it has to be done officially so there can't be an argument about who reported what to whom. You are?'

'Felipe García. And you want to know who my grandmother and great-grandmother were?'

'You have something to report?'

'I've just remembered.'

'What?'

'A man on the estate who wanted to know if someone called Kerr was around.'

'Did he say why he wished to know?'

'Seemed like he was angry.'

'When was this?'

Silence.

'Before Kerr died?'

'Yes.'

'Shortly before?'

'Yes.'

'Why haven't you reported this before?'

'Forgot.'

'Previously, I have asked if you'd ever noticed a stranger in the gardens shortly before the señor died when it was not an "open" day. You replied you had not.'

'Ain't I just said, I forgot?'

'What's reminded you?'

'You.'

'I'll ask again. What has recalled the incident to you? Did

something very recently occur which jogged your memory
because it had also happened just before or after you met the
man?'

'That's right.'

'What was it?'

'Don't remember.'

'Perhaps it was something like seeing a black vulture overhead after a long time when you hadn't seen one around?'

'That's right.'

'Can you describe this man?'

'Ordinary.'

'A foreigner?'

'Yes.'

'English?'

'Yes.'

'How do you know that? Did he try to speak Spanish?'

'No.'

'Proves he was English. Do you speak that language?'

'No.'

'So you couldn't talk to him?'

'Course I couldn't.'

'Then how did you understand what he wanted?'

'Kept saying "Kerr" and pointing at the house.'

'What did you do? Try to indicate with body movements
that there wasn't anyone but the family at home and he should
clear off?'

'Yes.'

'Is there anything more to tell me?'

'No.'

'Thank you for getting in touch.'

Alvarez looked at his watch. There was time to speak to
Salas. But as Agustín had written: better to consider well than
reconsider badly.

He phoned at six thirty.

'Yes?' Ángela Torres said curtly.

'Inspector Alvarez. Is the superior chief there?'

'Naturally.'

The connection was made. 'Yes?' demanded Salas.

'Inspector Alvarez reporting, señor. I have received a call from García who said—'

'Inform me who García is and what is the significance of his "call", by which I presume you mean that he phoned you.'

Seniors underlined their superiority both to their juniors and themselves by unnecessary officiousness. 'García is the gardener at Son Dragó. He has just reported that shortly before the death of the señor, he met a man on the estate who didn't speak Spanish or Mallorquin – García believes he was English – but managed to make it clear he wanted to know where Kerr was. His manner is described by García as angry. We may at last have learned that an as yet unidentified man had a stronger motive for the murder of Kerr than any other person.'

'You accept this report?'

'Yes, señor.'

'After days, weeks, of enquiries in which there has not been one mention of such an incident?'

'My immediate reaction, naturally, was to enquire into its possibility. Yet I had to come to the conclusion we cannot dismiss the evidence.'

'The interloper is supposed to have possessed a lethal dose of prussic acid?'

'Is there any basic difference from supposing the señora had one? García always made certain there were no bitter almonds around, and I have confirmed that fact. Suppose she found that for once he had not carried out his task as well as he should have done, how would she then use them to poison Kerr?'

'Persuade him to eat them.'

'He would have had to eat dozens to have had such a dramatic effect.'

'It fails to occur to you that probably she soaked and crushed them, then distilled the liquid to obtain the acid?'

'I'm afraid it does, señor.'

'What does?'

'It had failed to suggest itself to me. But would a woman have any understanding of how to do that?'

'There may be some with sufficient intelligence. Are you presuming the interloper was owed money by Kerr?'

'It seems the most likely—'

'He had five thousand euros in blackmail money and believed he would be able to continue blackmailing Señora Ashton.'

'If it was a drug deal . . .'

'From the beginning of this case, you have been unable to dismiss from your mind either drugs or elephants.'

'Señor, Kerr may have tried to steal from a dealer or shopped him, hoping for a reward, and this was the dealer's revenge. My impression is that García is telling the truth.'

'Facts are required, not impressions. You will question him again and demand answers which are at least vaguely credible.'

'As I mentioned, his evidence did initially trouble me, so I questioned him further and very thoroughly, especially on the points you have just raised. His evidence remained firm.'

'He must be questioned by someone possessed of skill, even though the victim was an Englishman and of a more than unwelcome character. I will request Inspector Domengue to fly over from Madrid to question García at midday, tomorrow. See García is here.'

'Señor, is that necessary when I doubt there is any further evidence to be gained?'

'A good reason to believe the contrary.'

'Was the meal so unappetizing?' Dolores asked Alvarez.

On his plate there remained a pork chop covered in a sauce made from milk, egg, olive oil, lemon juice, lard, parsley, pepper and salt.

'Perhaps I made a mistake. Did I forget the eggs?' she continued. 'But I am sure I cannot have done. However, one can only do one's best even when that is unappreciated.'

Jaime kicked Alvarez's ankle harder than intended. Alvarez yelped, as much from surprise as pain. 'What the hell are you doing?' he demanded as he reached down to rub his ankle.

'One must presume,' she said, 'that my husband was, in his own way, showing sympathy for me.'

'How does fracturing my ankle do that?'

'Understanding how long I spend in an overheated kitchen

– the fan has still not been repaired – how hard I try to provide a tasty meal no matter how exhausted I am, he is disturbed by your thoughtless manner.'

'What have I done now?'

'You have eaten hardly anything. Perhaps the dog next door will not be so particular about its diet.'

'It's a delicious *Costelles amb parallat*.'

'So delicious, you cannot bring yourself to eat more than a mouthful. However, since the rest of the family always enjoy their food, I will continue to try to please them.'

'I'm sorry . . .'

'As my mother used to say, apologizing is easier than avoiding the need to apologize.'

'I'm very worried.'

'She's checked the calendar?' Jaime suggested.

Dolores looked at him. Then, showing the concern she experienced when any family problem arose, she said quietly: 'What is wrong, Enrique?'

'Work,' Alvarez answered. 'I've taken one hell of a risk, and if Salas finds out . . . He'll get rid of me as if I had the plague.'

'What have you done?'

'Broken most of the rules.'

'Why?'

'If I hadn't, she was in danger of being either imprisoned or emotionally castrated.'

'When she's a woman?' Jaime asked.

'That you should think such a question does not surprise me,' she said. 'That you should ask it aloud, in front of the children, shocks me.'

Jaime hurriedly spoke to Alvarez. 'Is the problem because of the widow of the very wealthy Englishman from the bay?'

'Yes.'

'Is she Uncle's latest party piece?' Juan asked.

Dolores stood. 'There are times when my love for my family is sorely strained. Enrique, you will forgive my husband and son for their unthinking manners. Despite the many years I have tried to instil in them the need to act with kindness and understanding, I have failed. Do you wish to eat any more of your meal?'

'It really is delicious, but the worry has upset my stomach.'

'A man with a full stomach sheds his worries.'

'Your mother said that?' Jaime asked.

'I did. Enrique, give me your plate and I will warm up what you have left and, should you wish, you can finish it and also the little the others have left.'

Alvarez handed her his plate, and she carried it in to the kitchen.

'Even Einstein couldn't understand her,' Jaime muttered as he refilled his glass. 'She starts off saying what she thinks of you, ends up waiting on you hand and foot.'

Alvarez crossed to where García had just parked his Mobylette behind the garage at Son Dragó. 'You're late.'

'If you was paying the wages, I'd tell you why.'

'You're to be at the post in Llueso at midday tomorrow.'

'Why?'

'Inspector Domengue will question you about the man you saw on the estate shortly before Kerr was murdered.'

'I ain't talking to no one else.'

'You've no option unless you want to be found guilty of lying to the police.'

'I ain't said anything to anyone but you.'

'I am the police.'

For once, García found it difficult to say what he was thinking.

'Domengue has come from Madrid and my superior chief reckons he's very sharp. Being from there, he'll consider you to be an illiterate. Never hurts to help a man confirm his predetermined judgement.'

'Why can't you talk straight?'

Alvarez lit another cigarette. It might shorten his life by minutes, but anxiety and imagination was doing that by weeks. It was nearly five, and he still did not know how much García had been tricked into admitting. Suppose it had been every-thing? Unemployment was high except in the tourist season when there were temporary jobs for barmen, cooks, waiters, shop assistants . . . Would he be forced to find a job in a supermarket, telling holidaymakers Marmite was on the top shelf to the right of the second aisle, baked beans on the bottom shelf to the left of the fourth aisle?

The phone rang. He stubbed out the cigarette, reached for the receiver, hesitated. Until he answered the call, he remained an inspector.

'Yes,' he said, his voice hoarse.

'Alvarez, I have received a report from Inspector Domengue regarding his questioning of Felipe García,' Salas said.

Alvarez stared down at the bottom drawer in the desk. Alcohol soothed sorrow, healed wounds, overcame regrets.

'You have no interest in his report?'

'Of course I have, señor; very great interest. I was just wondering what it would be.'

'Inspector Domengue has, in his own words, never before questioned anyone so lacking in normal intelligence. When asked to describe the man who mentioned Kerr, García said he was about one metre seventy, but moments later, he was so tall it was like looking up at a tree; his hair was black, it was brown; he had a beard, then only a moustache. How did García know the man was angry and wanted to speak to Kerr when he couldn't understand English? He rushed into a flood of Mallorquin, which the inspector does not speak, as he tried to indicate what the man was doing, but looked as if he were imitating a windmill being blown to pieces. All the Inspector could determine was that the name Kerr was repeated several times and the man's manner showed considerable anger.'

'What is the inspector's conclusion, señor?'

'He would rather try to make sense of a four year old discussing the quantum theory.'

'Does he believe that García met a man on the estate shortly before Kerr died who clearly expressed reason to dislike Kerr?'

'In spite of all the garbled incoherence, that is the one point in García's evidence which he is prepared to accept. So you will identify this man.'

'Identify him?'

'That is what I said.'

'But with so little information, what chance is there of ever doing that?'

'None, if you start by accepting failure.'

'It's just that—'

'As efficient an interrogator as is Inspector Domengue, he has had little or no experience of questioning a typical Mallorquin of peasant background. In the circumstances, you are in a position to gather much more relevant information from García.'

'I will try my best, señor.'

'You will do better than that.'

'Even if I am unable to identify the trespasser, it is obvious Señora Ashton can no longer be considered a suspect.'

'You will leave me to determine such consideration.'

'You still think it possible she might be guilty when there is not a shred of evidence against her; when her guilt can only be provisionally accepted by assumptions for which, as you have made clear many times, you have a great dislike?'

Salas cut the connection.

Alvarez brought a bottle of Soberano and a glass out of the bottom drawer of the desk.